MW00577749

LYNDON JOHNSON
AND THE
MAJORETTES

DIFFICULTY AT THE BEGINNING

BOOK THREE

Keith Maillard

BRINDLE
& GLASS

SOUTH CHARLESTON PUBLIC LIBRARY
312 FOURTH AVENUE
SOUTH CHARLESTON, WV 25303-1297

Fic
Mall, K

180646

JUL 27 '06

Copyright © Keith Maillard 2006

All rights reserved. The use of any part of this publication reproduced, transmitted in
any form or by any means, electronic, mechanical, recording or otherwise, or stored in a
retrieval system, without the prior consent of the publisher is an infringement of the
copyright law. In the case of photocopying or other reprographic copying of the material,
a licence must be obtained from Access Copyright before proceeding.

Library and Archives Canada Cataloguing in Publication
Maillard, Keith, 1942-
Difficulty at the beginning / Keith Maillard.

Contents: bk. 1. Running — bk. 2. Morgantown —
bk. 3. Lyndon Johnson and the majorettes — bk. 4. Looking good.
ISBN 1-897142-06-4 (bk. 1).—ISBN 1-897142-07-2 (bk. 2).—
ISBN 1-897142-08-0 (bk. 3).—ISBN 1-897142-09-9 (bk. 4)

I. Title.

PS8576.A49D54 2005   C813/.54   C2005-903472-6

Cover images: Cloud: istockphoto.com, legs: Alamy Images
Author photo: Mary Maillard

Acknowledgements: LONG TALL TEXAN by Henry Strzelecki (pp. 1, 2, 7, 18, 21,
63, 64, 90, and 129) © March 2, 1959 ADAMS-ETHRIDGE PUBLISHING
COMPANY, transferred to and currently held by ISLE CITY MUSIC, ASCAP
International copyright secured. All rights reserved. Used by permission.

Canada Council   Conseil des Arts
for the Arts   du Canada

Brindle & Glass Publishing acknowledges the support of the Canada Council for the
Arts and the Alberta Foundation for the Arts for our publishing program.

Brindle & Glass Publishing
www.brindleandglass.com

Brindle & Glass is committed to protecting the environment and to the responsible
use of natural resources. This book is printed on 100% post-consumer recycled and
ancient-forest-friendly paper. For more information please visit www.oldgrowthfree.com.

1   2   3   4   5   09   08   07   06

PRINTED AND BOUND IN CANADA

ABOVE *The Abysmal, Water*

BELOW *The Arousing, Thunder*

Difficulty at the Beginning
works supreme success.

Lyndon Johnson
and the Majorettes
1965

I WAS hurrying to the afternoon shift when I heard that Jack Kennedy was dead. My first thought was, Jesus Christ, now we've got *Lyndon Baines Johnson!* I'd had the morning off. While I'd been sitting in the sun rubbing my hair with lemon juice and my skin with baby oil, Kennedy had been shot; he'd been pronounced dead by the time I got to the hotel. I was late for my shift as usual, and late for the drama, stepping cueless *in medias res* into that mummer's farce of busboys, waiters, and waitresses, even the cooks—the line between the restaurant staff and the customers dissolved as we all milled around in the dining room. Some people were jabbering frantically, some were crying, and I was stuck with Lyndon Johnson, that Southern asshole. All I knew of him was his public persona, cut from an old pop tune—I'M A LONG TALL TEXAN, RIDE A BIG WHITE HORSE—but that was enough to make me distrust him even more than other politicians, and I disliked and distrusted them all. I could never understand, except as metaphor, my old pal Revington's fascination with politics and power, the way he could turn JFK in the White House into a new age with new possibilities, "the winds of change," he used to say. And he was my next thought, emerging immediately on the boot heels of Texas Lyndon: Revington. Because he loved Kennedy, made much of him, and must even then be mourning him. Dead in Texas. *Texas!* I RIDE FROM TEXAS TO ENFORCE THE LAW.

Three years before, I'd been caught inadvertently by Kennedy's inaugural address while getting my hair cut to please my father. JFK had been declaiming away on the TV: ASK NOT WHAT YOUR COUNTRY CAN DO FOR YOU, ETC. My barber had paused, scissors in one hand, the other on my shoulder, to say, "Pretty good speech." A load of crap, I'd thought, and that's what I'd told Revington, leading to our most bitter argument in all the time I'd known him.

And my final thought, standing in my immaculately clean white busboy's uniform in the dining room of that posh Miami Beach hotel was this: *My God, I'm not in school anymore.* When the Confucians are in power, they always want you to take another test—another IQ test, or College Board Exam, or maybe a Graduate Placement Exam—and watch out, scholar, study hard or it will be a *physical exam* for the U. S. Army. Pretty soon there's not going to be a man-jack left in the country who's not in the service of the Emperor; Kennedy's dead in Dallas, Lyndon's on his way, and I no longer have a student deferment. HE'S COMING WITH A GUN AND HE JUST CAN'T BE BEAT.

When the Confucians are in power, the only sensible thing for Buddhists to do is retire to caves or mountains, so within days of the assassination, I was gone from Miami, on the road, my knapsack on my back, still chasing the vanishing white rabbit of Enlightenment. I dropped in unannounced on my friends and relatives—and distant friends of ever more distant friends and relatives—sustaining myself like Rilke's hero, each of my frequent downfalls (so I told myself) only a pretext for further existence, an ultimate rebirth. Riding my trusty thumb, I yo-yoed up and down the country from Cincinnati to Raysburg to Pittsburgh to New York to New Haven to Boston and points in between, but the only place I wouldn't go was back to Morgantown; the very thought of it filled me with horror. I worked, sometimes for no longer than a day, as a busboy, waiter, short-order cook, stock boy, night clerk, house painter, janitor, common laborer—any job I could get with no résumé, nary a reference, but plenty of bullshit. "I love this town, think I'll settle down here," I'd say to prospective employers, giving them my widest Alfred E. Newman grin even as I was planning my getaway. I found neither cave nor mountain.

Eventually I began to fear that I'd exhausted my career opportunities on the East Coast. I'd fallen in love with Raymond Chandler, so I rode the Greyhound to Los Angeles. The Chinese herbalist I visited there failed to take seriously my request for apprenticeship, but I conned my way into a job as a clerk in a seedy camera store on Sunset Boulevard (Chandler would have loved it) and decided that I really would settle down—at least long enough to write the great Civil War saga I'd been planning, the big fat book that would, once published, be the hottest thing since *Gone With the Wind*, and, without a doubt, be made into a major motion picture and establish me as one of the most promising young writers in America. I read Civil War histories, banged away on my typewriter, drank lots of beer, and ate. I swelled up until none of my clothes fit. I watched, on the snowy TV in my shadowy rented room, Texas Lyndon's invasion of the Dominican Republic. And, while plowing through a super deluxe banana split in a very famous drugstore in which someone once was discovered, I saw, walking in on the feet of an astonishingly beautiful girl—a long-legged, iconic, and exquisitely self-possessed girl (a starlet, surely)—the very first pair of white go-go boots ever worn in North America.

Just as I'd always feared that I would, I ended up back in Raysburg dead broke and out to lunch. It was the summer of sixty-five. I hadn't been home in over a year. All Revington could talk about was politics: "Johnson's turning into a damn fine president."

"He's an asshole."

"Come on, Dupre, what about Selma?"

"What *about* Selma? He only did what any sane president would do. What about the Dominican Republic?"

"What do you want down there, another Cuba?"

And from Cassandra: "Will you guys cut the crap."

The last time I'd seen Cassandra, she'd been playing the role of Canden High teen queen for all it was worth; a year at Bennington had changed her once again, stripped away any vestiges of her earlier personae, pared her down to an austere sexiness, and left her, so it appeared, with a *Weltanschauung* of unrelieved bleakness. She was dressed that night as she would be most other nights that summer—in glove-tight jeans and a boy's white shirt. Her thick burnt-sienna hair was parted in the center of her forehead and hung, curling languidly on its own, halfway down her back. She outlined her wide-set eyes with fine black lines (carefully defining even the tear ducts), coated her lashes with inky mascara, used cover-up for lipstick, and (largely, I suspected, to appear *outré* in Raysburg), painted her fingernails dead white. When I was being honest with myself, I admitted that I'd always been in love with her.

Now, from where I was sitting, I could look across to the mirror behind the bar, see the three of us brooding in a booth like the characters in a Cubist painting, our images fractured into facets between the whiskey bottles. I imagined I could see myself getting fatter by the minute. "What are we going to do?" Revington said, assuming one of his quoting voices. "What are we *ever* going to do . . . pressing lidless eyes and waiting for a knock upon the door?"

"A game of chess?" I said, picking it up.

"He's dead," from Cassy.

"Yeah, I heard that," I said.

"Let's drink to him," Revington said, raising his glass. "Here's to you, Thomas Stearns, and to your magnificent obscurity. Long may you puzzle university freshmen."

"Yes," I said, "here's to you, master of the mug's game. You defined our age."

"Thanks for the footnotes," Cassandra said.

We drank to T. S. Eliot.

"Now what?" I said.

"We could drive to Pittsburgh," Revington said.

"What the hell's in Pittsburgh?"

"I don't know. We haven't got there yet."

"Maybe there's a good movie on," Cassy said.

"We'd never make it in time," Revington said, looking at his watch, then brightening, "unless I drove like hell."

"That's reason enough," I said. "Let's put it on the road."

Outside, the wet heat engulfed us as palpably as if we'd stepped into an ocean of simmering mucilage. I began to sweat. The clock on the bank told us that it was ten minutes of eight, the thermometer that it was ninety-two degrees. I'd been back in town less than a week, and already it felt like a life sentence. "Isn't it ever going to rain in this fucking place?" I said.

"It can't stay at ninety-nine point ninety-nine percent humidity forever," Revington said. "Eventually the whole valley's going to supersaturate, and we'll all drown."

Overhead the nighthawks were pursuing insects across the bland cloudless sky. The damn birds were yelling their heads off. "Hey, do you guys really want to go to Pittsburgh?" I asked.

"Shit, no," from Cassy.

"So what the fuck are we going to do?" from Revington.

"Going to the river," I intoned, "going to take my rocking chair . . ."

Just as I'd wanted him to, Revington fell in with me and we chanted the rest of it in unison: "If the blues overtake me, going to rock away from here."

"Oh, for Christ's sake," Cassandra said.

"Any beer left at your place?" he asked her, and then, like an evangelist, thrust his arms straight up into the steamy air. "Ah, that it should come to this!"

I looked at him, Revington, handsome lad with his Italian loafers and razor-cut hair and pressed chinos, and I thought how oddly the wheel had turned for us. When I'd been on the Dean's List at WVU, *he'd* been the peripatetic fuck-up, but now he was the one who'd managed to screw out his Bachelor of Arts degree and was off to Harvard Law School in the fall. He'd even managed to get himself affianced to the granddaughter of a goddamn senator. Her name was Alicia (Revington poured the syllables of it through his mouth like syrup: Ah-Lee-Sha); she has wonderful taste, he told me; she dressed beautifully. She was sensitive, loved children, was a *real woman*—and reasonably intelligent to boot! And now *I* was the one, my Dean's List days long gone, who'd fucked up, had dropped out of school with my mind in tatters, who didn't have a degree in anything and wasn't about to be getting one, who didn't have a girlfriend, elegant or otherwise, who, if the truth were told, hadn't even touched a girl since Morgantown: a fat, broke, horny, unemployed, draft-eligible, Buddhist Confederate. And Revington, Cassandra, and I were rolling through this vile hot night, across the Ohio River, over Raysburg Hill, to Meadowland and Cassy's house.

Zoë met us at the door. She'd long ago stopped wearing Cassandra's clothes, and she'd never had Cassandra's taste. Her hair had been set and brushed into a swingy teenage pageboy with bangs that met her eyebrows; she wore the kind of simple little dress the fashion mags were calling a "skimmer" and, to complete the Young London Look, white go-go boots fetched down from Pittsburgh in the spring—her pride and joy. "Real kid," she'd told us, "not this plastic junk that's showing up in town now."

Looking at her, I found myself generating a mad conceit: strange the inevitability of process in America. Back when our presence in Vietnam had been "advisory," my Hollywood drug-store starlet must have bought her go-go boots in England or France, and God knows how much she'd paid for them; last winter when U.S. bombers first began to pound North Vietnam, the boots (by Herbert Levine) were advertised in *Vogue* for a hundred and fifty dollars a pair; by March, when we sent in the Marines, you could, like Zoë, buy them at Bergdorf Goodman's for fifty bucks; by summer, we had seventy thousand U.S. personnel in Vietnam, were flying over six hundred bombing sorties a week over the north, and go-go boots could be had at Sears for $10.95; now Johnson was talking of increasing our commitment to a hundred and twenty-five thousand men, and every girl in town looked like a majorette. I RIDE FROM TEXAS ON A BIG WHITE HORSE. "Ah, Zoë," Revington was saying in his best Gregory Peck manner, "you look stunning, as usual."

Zoë had long ago grown accustomed to Cassy's male friends, their teasing, their ridiculous comments. She paid Revington absolutely no attention, but his choice of words had not been ridiculous at all; she *was* stunning. I much preferred the dark intri-cacies of Cassandra's beauty, but I suspected that most boys would not agree with me. Zoë had always been a very pretty little girl, but while I'd been gone, she'd been wonderfully transformed—had shot up to be a good two inches taller than her sister and had grown magnificent long legs that would have done any majorette proud. If she was still something of a gawky kid, she was a gawky kid who just happened to look exactly right for the times. Now she was prancing and chattering, dragging Cassandra along behind her, to the center (I gathered) of some immense and exciting project.

From the living room Doctor Markapolous called out, "Hey

there, boys," to Revington and me. As I followed Cassy following Zoë, I saw the good doctor laid out in his usual manner before the educational TV channel, his pipe in his lap and his newspapers piled up by his chair. He sent us a wave, a gesture of invitation. Revington grinned, stepped toward him (picking up the gage), while I, sniffing titillation, trailed after the girls, headed downstairs to the recreation room—little sister's territory.

Zoë had spread the basement with fabric—gay colors, a Fauve's palette; it looked as though every skirt and dress she owned was piled up there. At the center of things was her sewing machine, waiting, while, on the radio, the Beatles were telling us that they felt fine. "I finished it," Zoë was squealing at her sister.

"Great," Cassy said, "let's see it on you."

"You really want to?"

"Of course I really want to."

Zoë shot upstairs. "She sees something in a magazine she likes," Cassandra told me, "she copies it. Doesn't even need the pattern, just something close." I could hear in her voice a sisterly mixture of annoyance, amusement, and affection. "She's a lot better than I ever was."

Zoë was back in an instant, wearing a white dress—very simple, very white, and very short, the hemline at mid-thigh. She strutted in a circle around us, showing herself off. Cassandra was laughing, "My God, Zo, you'll get arrested." But dresses exactly like that had been in all the magazines for at least a year. "Terrific," I said. "It looks like a Courrèges."

"Oh, good," Zoë said, clapping her hands, "that's what it's supposed to look like."

"Where on earth do you think you're going to wear it?" Cassandra said.

"I didn't make it to wear anywhere. It's for my book."

"Yeah, your *book*. Right."

"Don't make fun of me, Cassy. I'm serious."

"Believe me, little sister, I know you're serious."

"But I *am* going to shorten all my skirts."

"Oh, I wouldn't do that," Cassandra said dryly.

Frisky Zoë trotted about, grabbing up magazines, riffling through them to show us. "Look. Do you see how short some of them are? See? Here. Look at this one. Isn't it cute? It's how they're wearing them *in England*," and then to me: "How are the girls wearing them in L.A.?"

"Short," I said. "Really short. The high-school girls anyway. They're all above the knee. Some of them are really really short."

"Oh, Raysburg's so out of it! How short do you think I can go?" She drew an imaginary line an inch above her knee.

"Sure," I said.

"Oh, for Christ's sake," her sister said. "Don't listen to him; he's a dirty old man . . . Seriously, Zo, don't shorten everything. That's what they want you to do. Then they'll drop the hemlines, and you'll have to buy a whole bunch of new skirts."

"Listen, kid," I said, annoyed with Cassandra for *dirty old man*, "I'm in touch with the *Zeitgeist*, so you can take it from me. Skirts are going nowhere but up."

"See," Zoë said triumphantly, "John knows. He's been in L.A."

"Yeah," Cassy said, giving me a wicked smile, "when it comes to skirts, John knows it all. Why don't you get *him* to take your pictures. He's a photographer."

"Worked in a camera store," I corrected her.

"Oh, would you?" Zoë said. "That'd be so cool."

"All I did was take passport photos," I said, but they weren't listening to me.

"Here, let me show you my book," Zoë said.

She handed me what looked like a slim leather briefcase, but I'd seen enough of these things to know what it was: a fancy portable photo album that camera stores sold to aspiring young models for far too much money. I opened it and looked at her pictures. There were a few professional eight-by-tens that certified Zoë as a lovely girl indeed, but, as photographs go, none of them was better than small-town mediocre. There were half a dozen more that looked exactly like what they were: blown-up snapshots taken by her dad; the best that could be said of them was "cute." Her book wasn't much—even by the fairly low standards I had for comparison, but I said, "Very nice, Zoë. It's a good start."

Sitting behind the counter in a camera store on Sunset Boulevard, I'd seen plenty of books. I'd never understood why the girls carried them around. "That's how they know they're models," Mr. Feinstein told me. He'd owned the place for thirty years; he'd seen it all. "If you're a model, you got a book. If you got a book, you carry it around." The girls came in for head shots. Mr. Feinstein took them into the dirty little back room where he kept a roll of seamless, a stool, and the lights set up and ready to go. "You're beautiful, kid," he'd murmur at them in his gravelly Brooklyn voice. "You're a knockout, baby, I swear to God," and they always fell for it; the plainest little Jane from the Midwest would instantly be smiling back at the lens as though the love of her life were on the other side of it. "I feel sorry for them," Mr. Feinstein told me. "If they're getting their head shots from the back of a camera store, they're going nowhere." He thought most people in L.A. were going nowhere. He was right.

I followed the girls back upstairs. Zoë was chattering about Courrèges' space girls, Mary Quant's show in New York, the clubs in London, THE LOOK. "Oh, Zoë, it's too short!" her mother wailed at her.

"It's for her book," Cassy said in a deadpan voice. I helped myself to a beer.

"You know, Cass," Zoë was saying, "if you cut bangs in your hair, you'd look like Françoise Hardy."

"Oh, for Christ's sake."

"Cassandra, your language," from Mom.

Cassandra followed me into the living room, saying under her breath, "*Cassandra, your language* . . . Oh, Christ. Between Zoë and the old woman, I don't know whether I'm coming or going in this goddamned house . . . They both keep wanting to make me over. Françoise Hardy, for fuck's sake."

We walked into an argument so good that Cassy's dad had turned off the tube. Revington was blathering about "our overseas commitments." He sounded like Lyndon Johnson's press secretary. Doctor Markapolous was replying with the French, Dien Bien Phu, the Bao Di, Vietnam's traditional distrust of China, and the stupidity of the bombing. He sounded like *The New York Review of Books*. I'd heard it all before. "I'm sick of this crap," I said. "We've got no business in Vietnam in any capacity whatsoever, and there's no point in talking about how we got there. All we should be talking about is how fast we can get the hell out." I'd stopped both of them in mid-flight, and, now that I had their attention, I wanted to tack on something mad and outrageous. "We're collecting the karma from the War of Secession."

Revington gave me a look that said, as clearly as if he'd sent it by telegram, "Oh, you shithead," but the doctor, always eager for a new point of view, said, "What's that, John? What are you saying?"

"It's that goddamn Yankee meddling again. It's what's built this country. Yankee meddling. If there's somebody somewhere who isn't just like you, you've got to convert them. If you can't convert them, then you kill them. And you institute the draft so you'll have enough cannon fodder, and you fight the bloodiest war in American history to wipe out the last hope of regionalism, to force a centralized urbanized monolith down the throat of the South . . ." and I felt myself swelling out to full Confederate oratorical rotundity: "with a thirty-year Reconstruction called thorough, and *thorough* it was in every sense of the word, carried on with Yankee bayonets, carried on in a manner maybe two cuts above the Nazis, and you create a defeated, screwed-up people with night in their souls. But you keep the Union together . . . that machine. And you're off for Manifest Destiny, for the Philippines . . . and for Vietnam. And now you've got a *Southern* asshole in the White House, the kind of Southerner the Yankees made, with night in his soul. And he's been sent there to pay back the karma. He thinks he's going to reconstruct Vietnam, but what he's going to do is divide the United States right down the middle, the way it hasn't been divided since 1861."

The good doctor is doing his best to understand my hemorrhage of words. Am I talking about states' rights? If the Southern states had maintained their rights in the Civil War, they would have maintained slavery. If they had those rights now, they'd maintain segregation. What would be the good in that? He's giving me a puzzled look—ah, this younger generation—while Revington, who knows me, is saying, "Oh, hell, he's not defending slavery. It's just Dupre's silly fantasy. He wishes we had a dozen small ineffective nations here instead of one powerful one."

"You're goddamned right," I said, "a loose confederation . . . Swiss Cantons . . . anything but this centralized juggernaut."

I'd long ago stopped caring for facts, for sound arguments, for seeing the justice of a position; all I was trying to do was articulate a vision growing in me: waste and damnation. "Christ," I said, "Vietnam makes me sick . . . It's like that speech crazy Mario Savio made: there comes a time finally when it just makes you so sick you've got to lie down on the machinery . . ."

"Oh, Mario Savio?" Revington said. "Come on, Dupre. When they write the history books, who do you think they're going to remember? That little drop-out demagogue Savio or a man like Clark Kerr who's written an incisive analysis of the university?"

"They're not going to remember either of them particularly," Doctor Markapolous said, nailing his words into the air with his pipe stem, "You understand? Both of them will be lucky to make the history books at all. What they will say is that in the mid-sixties great changes began to take place in America . . ."

"No," said Revington, "no great changes. Every generation's thought that. A time of great change. No. Things will continue the way they have been. Change will be gradual the way it always has been . . . and should be in a democracy. At the core things will stay the same . . . the political process . . ." ASK NOT, ETC. He unfolded himself and stretched. "I'm going home and take a shower," he announced, and with a cavalier wave he was gone.

"I don't know about your friend William Revington," the good doctor said. "He's made peace with himself too soon. I don't understand. I'm fifty-four years old. *I'm* supposed to be the conservative in this outfit."

CASSANDRA AND I sat in the dark on the front porch glider and offered ourselves to the mosquitoes. "Oh, Jesus," she said, "I don't know how much longer I can stand it. Every day it's the same fucking thing. Wake up and it's a hundred and fifty degrees. And it never rains. And we're all going to do the same goddamn thing we did yesterday . . . *nothing*. We're going to lay around the house, or have a beer, or drive over to Ohio to have a beer. And

13

my crazy menopausal mother will change her clothes fourteen times, all the way down to her underwear. And Zoë will be copying another dress out of a magazine, or shortening her skirts, or driving around with her boyfriend playing kissy face. And William will drop by, and he'll be as full of shit as he was the day before. And the old man will be parked in front of the tube, and he and William will argue about Vietnam. And now that you're back in town, you can join the show. Jesus, it's all so boring. Have you got a cigarette?"

I pounded one out of the pack and passed it to her. "Yeah," I said, "I don't know why I came back here."

She gave me a somber, intensely focused look, then looked away. "I don't know why you did either."

I was stung. What the hell had she meant by that? Would she have preferred it if I hadn't come back?

"I wish I could get my head shaved," she said, lifting her hair clear of her neck. "This fucking hair's stifling me." Her neck was wet with perspiration; her shirt was soaked with it.

In the old days I would have simply asked her what she'd meant and she would have told me in that absolutely straightforward way of hers, but now I couldn't bring myself to say a word. I never would have imagined that I would have trouble talking to Cassandra. *She*, of course, had been the main reason I'd come back to Raysburg, but I'd already been home for over a week, and I still hadn't connected with her in any kind of real way. I had to shuffle through the deck of possibilities in my mind to find the next thing to say: "So when did Zoë start this modeling stuff?"

"Last fall. Christ, it's a crime the way they fill those little girls' minds up with shit. Dad let her take this Mickey Mouse modeling course for teenagers last fall . . . just to shut her up . . . but that led to Level Two . . . you know, for the really *serious* girls, the really *talented* girls. And Level Two cost a hell of a lot more, of course, and then there was Level Three, and that one cost the national debt. Dad said he'd be damned if he was going to pay for it, so she went to Mom and said, 'Oh, Mommy, puhleeze. I have to. I just have to. It's my *career!*' You should see all the makeup they sold her. She keeps it in a goddamn tackle box."

I laughed. "And of course there's plenty of job opportunities here in Raysburg."

"Yeah, it's ridiculous. Even Zoë knows better than that. She's going to New York, she says, as soon as she's out of high school. You can imagine how much Dad likes hearing that one, but . . . I don't know. Who the hell am I to dump on her? She's not laying around here day after day bored out of her fucking mind."

She slumped back in the glider, put her feet up on the railing; it was a characteristic posture for her, one that plunged me instantly into a thick soup of melancholic nostalgia: ah, the miraculous and lost summer of 1960 when we'd first met—ah, the miraculous and lost summer of 1961 when we'd made out night after night like a pair of lovesick ferrets. She was wearing the little black lace-up shoes that completed her evening uniform. They fit her as tightly as ballet slippers, and she wore them without socks, had worn them so much that the shapes of her little toes were clearly outlined in the soft leather. I wanted to say, "Where the hell have you gone, Cassy?" but I didn't.

OK, I thought, we've done Zoë, now let's do Revington. "You think William's really going to marry the senator's granddaughter?"

"Oh, hell, I don't know. It gives him something to do."

"What's she like? You've met her, haven't you?"

"Ah-Lee-Sha? Sure, I've met her. William brought her up here over spring break. She's . . . I couldn't believe she was for real . . . OK, she's a little ice blond via her hairdresser. Very much the lady.

Great figure. Great clothes. And the accent . . . my God, you should hear it. This mush-mouthed molasses bullshit, and . . . Oh, Christ, the country-club set. Horses. Tennis. She goes to Hollis. Her girl friends call her 'Lissy.' She's like one of Fitzgerald's characters . . . I think in *The Great Gatsby* . . . the one who looks like she's always balancing something fragile on the tip of her chin."

"Hey, that's a good one. And she's really a senator's grand-daughter?"

"Oh, you better believe it. Their whole family's involved in politics. You know how things are downstate . . . crooked as a dog's hind leg. And William just loves it. Thinks he's staring right into the heart of the American political system. And God knows, he probably is."

"I don't know how he does it. I could have lived my whole life and never even *met* a senator's granddaughter."

"Oh, sure you know how he does it. He's *a Revington*. He met her at some fucking country-club dance . . . you know, a cotillion or some damn thing . . . and then he's *so goddamned sexy*."

I shot my cigarette away into the dark. "I'm going home," I said. "Maybe I can read or something."

DRIVING MY mother's old clunker Dodge over Raysburg Hill back to the Island, I was, once again, reciting my private litany: *Oh, this is intolerable, intolerable.* I wasn't sure I knew Cassandra anymore. Yes, just who was it that was hiding out now behind the smart-ass persona, looking out at the world with penetrating grey eyes ringed with fine black lines like a cat's? Nobody at nineteen could be quite as jaded, bored, cynical, worldly-wise, and damn well existentially *flattened* as she appeared to be at the moment, so it had to be a consciously chosen role, but always before she'd invited me backstage to discuss the nuances of her performance, and now I felt firmly excluded. I used to think I was closer to Cassandra than anybody. At dawn at the top of North High Street in Morgantown we'd stepped outside of time—by God, we'd fused together like the two halves of Plato's egg—but was that moment of mystical union still as precious to her as it was to me? She'd only been sixteen, and I hadn't done very well at keeping in touch since then—and, of course, I'd come back to Raysburg looking like Fatty Arbuckle's little brother.

I parked the car in front of my parents' apartment, but I couldn't bring myself to go inside yet. I should never have come back to Raysburg. Oh, this is intolerable, intolerable. Going nowhere, I wandered up Front Street headed for the bridge. Dealing out the choices of my life like so many cards, laying them down with a snap like the riverboat gambler in my novel. GO BACK TO MORGANTOWN IN THE FALL. What, go back to the place where I lost my goddamn mind? OK, DON'T GO BACK TO MORGANTOWN. STAY IN RAYSBURG AND GET A JOB. What job? Stay in Raysburg and get drafted is more like it. OK, SO GET DRAFTED. ASK NOT WHAT YOUR COUNTRY CAN DO FOR YOU, ETC. Are you kidding? WELL THEN, APPLY FOR CONSCIENTIOUS OBJECTOR STATUS. As what religion? Buddhist? "And just exactly which temple do you attend, Mr. Dupre?" BE A HERO, THE MAR-TYRED PACIFIST, GO TO JAIL. Screw that!

But in the meantime: Oh, this is intolerable, intolerable. What it comes down to, finally, is not getting through the rest of my life, but merely surviving the rest of the summer: how am I going to get through *tonight*? A cold six-pack in the refrigerator and rock 'n roll on the radio and the excellent Mr. Cash's *The Mind of the South*? The latest issue of *Vogue*? And Revington is *sexy*, is he? The bastard. Pulling that one out, finally: even

Cassandra thinks he's sexy, and, goddamn it, he's always been sexy, always had that sense of command—one of *the* Revingtons—and now he's perfecting it: I RIDE FROM TEXAS ON A BIG WHITE HORSE. Girls must like it. And suddenly, here are girls, as I look up from my preoccupation to find myself passing through a bevy of them; they're hurrying, giggling, out too late, homeward: a gaggle of them as alike as if they'd been issued uniforms—blouses, shorts, and white go-go boots—pubescent majorettes. Hey mister, IS THAT YOUR HORSE? Revington's dry edgy voice in my ear: "Ciao, Marcello." I hadn't seen him coming; he'd pulled over next to me, was leaning out the window of the car, posed, with a cigarette dangling from his lips. It didn't feel a bit like coincidence.

"Evening, William," I said, walked around to the passenger's side and got in. "Another lovely evening in beautiful Raysburg, Queen of the Panhandle."

"Indeed," he said, putting the car in gear.

"How'd you find me?"

"Elemental. Your car was at your place, but your mom said you weren't. Where else would you be?"

We were aimed right back to the bar in Ohio where we'd started. "What is this Confederate crap, Dupre?" Revington was saying; "you're not any more of a Confederate than I am."

"It's my novel," I said. "If you're writing about Confederates, you've got to think like one. And while we're on the subject of playing the role, how did you turn into such a fucking hawk?"

He laughed, then intoned, "They had their Spanish Civil War, we have our Vietnam . . . Yeah, so much for glory."

As he drove, I looked over at him, at his profile; yes, he was as handsome as an actor. "Something honorable," he muttered, a line from *Lawrence of Arabia* he'd been quoting ever since we'd seen the movie. "Yeah, John, I know it's a stupid war. God knows, I know it. But shit, Johnson's doing the best he can. He inherited a mess . . ."

"Crap."

"Yeah. I know what you think, but I don't agree. He's a consummate politician. He's not going to make any more mistakes than he has to."

"Crap, again."

"Fuck, let's not get into that. It's just that I've been thinking . . . Well, sometimes it comes down to tradition . . . something honorable, you know? And there's been a Revington in every war this country's ever fought."

Though his voice had been heavy with melodrama, I felt that I had, finally, heard something from close to the heart of him. "Maybe," I said, "this will be the first one without a Revington."

"I'm not so sure. I keep thinking, what the hell business have I to go merrily off to law school? I should be in uniform."

"Oh Jesus, man."

"And then I think it's not going to make any difference anyway. Pretty soon we're all going to be in uniform whether we like it or not."

"Oh shit, they're not going to draft you out of law school."

"Don't be too sure of that, Dupre. We'll both be in by winter."

"I won't," I said.

"I don't see how you're going to avoid it."

I didn't answer him. I wasn't sure how I was going to avoid it either. "Did your family really fight for the Confederacy?" he asked suddenly.

I laughed. "Well, that depends on who you believe. My father always claimed that the First John Henry Dupre . . . after he'd killed a man in a knife fight down in New Orleans . . . or maybe it was a gun fight . . . anyhow, the story was that he came up to Kentucky and rode with Morgan. You know, John Hunt Morgan, the famous Confederate raider? But then again, my old man might have made the whole thing up . . . But on my mother's side there's no doubt. My great-grandfather Wheelwright," I said slowly, "was a drummer in the Ohio National Guard."

"A what?"

"A drummer. You know, fuckhead, he beat on a drum."

Revington began to chuckle. "And in the *Ohio* National . . ."

"Yeah, in the Ohio National Guard," I said flatly.

He burst into laughter. "Oh, Jesus, man, he beat the drum for the Union."

"Shhhh," I said, putting my finger to my lips, "don't tell anyone."

"Oh, that's beautiful. That really is. That's why I like you, Dupre, that's why we're friends. We're both such fucking poseurs."

Coming into it out of the hot night, I found the cool bar such a relief that I settled down to stay there till it closed. "This fucking town is driving me nuts," Revington said, "and Alicia's in Europe till the end of the month." Ah-Lee-Sha.

"That must be nice for her."

"Yeah, she was so excited to cross the great water. Just like a little kid. It was touching . . . It's supposed to 'broaden her horizons,' but I think her parents just wanted to split us up for a while," and then, in a voice that was a parody of a radio soap opera: "to see if our *love is real.*"

"That sounds positively Victorian."

"They're like that. It took me a while to believe *they're* for real." He grinned at me. "Hey, do you want to see some pictures?"

He pulled an envelope out of his back pocket, withdrew some Kodacolor snaps, and spread them on the table before me, fanning them out like cards. Alicia with her parents, Alicia alone, Alicia with Revington. The wind was blowing through Revington's hair; he already looked the part of the young lawyer. Alicia wore what appeared to be an expensive suit: beautifully cut, young but not outrageous (the skirt just skimming the tops of her kneecaps), and, of course, white go-go boots, the *Vogue* hundred-and-fifty dollar pair I suspected; now that they'd made it down to the level of Sears, I was sure that she wouldn't be caught dead in them. Money, I thought, she's used to lots of it. That's what will keep Revington on the straight and narrow. A beautiful girl to be sure, one of Lyndon's majorettes. It felt like a trap to me (I RIDE FROM TEXAS TO ENFORCE THE LAW), but I was so envious of Revington's sure charted life, of his classy girlfriend, that I was momentarily sick with it, nauseated. "Very nice," I said.

He retrieved the pictures, folded them away. "I miss her," he said, a far gaze in his eyes. "Sometimes I think I'd like to get her pregnant before I go . . ."

"Go where?"

He pointed vaguely toward the bar, conjuring up the jungles of Vietnam. "I think the British fliers must have felt like that," he said in his World War II movie voice. "They knew they weren't going to come back . . . wanted to leave something of themselves behind for the world . . . something honorable . . . a baby."

I was so angry with him I couldn't even laugh. I lit a cigarette. "Get off it, Revington. You're not going anywhere except to law school."

"No, Dupre. That's not our destiny any longer. We're all going to be in uniform . . . the entire generation."

"Revington, what the hell's happened to you? You used to be so crazy."

MY MEMORIES of him were as clear as any of the snapshots he'd just showed me. When, scared witless, I'd first appeared at the Raysburg Military Academy, Revington had been the only one of my classmates who'd bothered to talk to me. What the already supremely self-assured class wise-ass could have seen in shy, bookish, painfully thin (and still somewhat girlish) me, I was never sure, but he soon won me with his talent for imitating movie actors, politicians, and our teachers, for quoting great sluices of rhetoric from Shakespeare to Winston Churchill. He'd call me up and announce himself: "Hello, this is William Revington," his delivery a trenchant drawl, half Rhett Butler, half British Intelligence. Then I'd begun to imitate him, echoing back in the same tones, "Hello, this is John Dupre." Until finally, he'd begun to imitate me imitating him. As we'd become close friends, we'd cultivated these privately convoluted routines—reflections of reflections.

It's Christmas vacation a few years back. I'm still at WVU, and Revington is still nominally at Yale, although he hasn't set foot in New Haven in quite a while. We're sitting in a young lady's living room. It doesn't matter which particular young lady; she's merely one of Revington's female audiences.

Alone with me, he speaks of his tours of America in a wry self-deprecating way, making himself the butt of every joke, a goofy Li'l Abner stumbling through an ominous Burroughsian world. It's a man-to-man tone; he knows full well that I will supply the unstated heroism. But now, for public consumption, his manner is altered. He is staring glassily at the wall. He's just blown into town, has been awake for twenty-four hours, and "Shit, I'm not sleeping much these days anyway . . ." dismissing the concept of sleep with a pushing gesture, Camel cigarette in hand, fingers stained brown to the knuckle. Glancing at me, he deposits, in parenthesis, "They say in the last few months of his life that

Modigliani was seen to be heavily salting all the food he ate." Pause. "It scared the shit out of me when I read it. I've been piling salt on everything." And he throws *that* away with the same laconic gesture. He's talking about New York; he and a friend ("a beautiful lost sensitive madman") had been stopped by a Negro pimp in Times Square. A detective had come over and asked the pimp to stand against the wall. "It was like a play that had been rehearsed too many times," he's saying, "rehearsed over and over again until the actors are totally bored." He falls silent, as though *he* has become totally bored. His eyes fuse over again; he's left us, to visit what land of Boschian horrors or delights we can only speculate.

"William?" the young lady says. No reaction. "William?"

He snaps around to look at her. "Oh, sorry . . . that seems to be happening to me a lot lately. Sorry . . . What was I saying?" He's off again, pronouncing these magic names resonant with numina: The Port Authority, Harlem, The A Train, The Thalia, The Fat Black Pussy Cat. Now he is telling us that a model from *Seventeen* bought him lunch. "I hate to drop names," he says, giving me a weighted look, "but she lives on Bleeker Street." And he's gone again.

"William? William!"

"What? . . . Oh, sorry . . ."

"Have you been drinking?" she asks him.

"Ask John how much I've had to drink."

"Not a drop," I say, playing the straight man, as always.

In a fatigued voice he begins to explain to her that he is tired, begins to tell her exactly what he has been doing that has made him so tired. His tiredness, his lassitude, his exhaustion is tremendous, but he will muster the effort to tell her about it; he will exhaust himself still further in the search for the origins of the exhaustion, knowing all the while that the enterprise is futile.

Dull girl, she can't perceive the beauty of the performance, interrupts to ask, "Have you seen Barbara?" That's his old high-school girlfriend, "that wench," as he calls her.

"This disturbs me," he says wearily. "Everybody's trying to hang onto the good old days . . . the good old friendships. Emotionally she's still in high school. When will she realize that she's got to accept a quiet mundane existence? She's probably rolling around in an alley right now, dead drunk. Yes . . . she's smashed. She's throwing beer bottles at the moon and listening to them break. She's tilting them back and letting the beer run through her hair . . ."

"Oh, William, you know she's at the Oval, perfectly all right."

"She's stewed," he says dogmatically. "I just don't want to play games anymore. I played games with her for years. I just don't want to do it anymore. She's got to accept an ordinary life . . . and I . . . I've got to move on."

Good show, I think. Dean Moriarity. Yes, yes!

NOW I looked at him across the table: that lean face I knew so well. We'd gone through a lot together. "Remember how you used to stagger down the streets of Morgantown dead drunk, yelling the opening lines from *Howl*?" I said.

"Yeah," he said.

"The only time I've ever got stoned in my life was with you, asshole . . . when you showed up with that little bag of tea in your boot, twenty-four hours on the road from Boston."

"That's right," he said, laughing. "It was a fucking bleak time, but there was something beautiful in it." He grimaced. "It's not easy, John, you know that?"

"What?"

"Growing up. Shit, you can't stay twenty forever."

"But you don't have to be forty before you're thirty."

He grinned. "Is that what you think I'm doing?"

"Yeah, that's what I think you're doing."

"I don't know . . . but I think I'm finally on the right track now. If I can bring to politics something of what Kennedy meant to me . . ." His eyes glazed over the way they used to in the old days; then he came back, looked at me sharply: "How the hell did you get so fat? I think you're fucking off, John. I think you're drifting."

"You're goddamn right I'm drifting," I told him, and I launched into fabulous tales of my drift. The high-proof Ohio beer was flowing nicely, and we helped it along from time to time with shots of Irish whiskey (Hemingway's drink, Revington said, and he was paying for everything by then). I told him the story of the demon trucker who'd driven me from Huntington to Morgantown—but I moved it up in time and changed its location, inserted it into my trip to the west coast. Although I'd ridden the Greyhound to L.A., I told him I'd hitchhiked there. Although my guitar was gathering dust in my parents' place on the Island, I told him I'd pawned it in Denver—so we could chant together (along with Kerouac): "Down in Denver, down in Denver, all I did was die!"

"Why the hell'd you go to L.A.?" he asked me.

I couldn't believe how beautifully he'd set me up. "My health," I said in my flattest Bogart voice. "I went to L.A. for the waters."

He got it instantly: "Waters? What waters? There's no waters in L.A."

Howling with laughter, we screamed out the next line in unison: "I WAS MISINFORMED."

"You want to know what L.A. was like?" I said. "I'll give you the perfect metaphor for what L.A. was like."

25

What I told him was a true story, although I can't say that I didn't embellish it a little around the edges. There'd been a particularly bleak period during my stay in the City of Angels when I ate all of my meals in a restaurant directly across from where I was living ("I hate to drop names," I told him) on *Sunset Boulevard*. It was one of those big fancy-ass glass-front drive-ins that never closed, and I loved the place. "Clean and well-lighted?" Revington said.

"You got it," I said. And even if I stayed up half the night working on my Civil War novel, I knew that food was always available—a great consolation to me. I ate the same thing at every meal: a hot turkey sandwich with gravy. I liked the ritual of it.

One night around four in the morning, a girl came in and sat down next to me. She was pretty enough, late teens or early twenties, scrawny as a plucked chicken, with an antique look about her as though she'd stepped out of a high-school annual from the fifties: a weirdly convoluted hairdo with kiss curls, a little blue dress with puff sleeves and a droopy skirt. The dress had stains down the front and looked as though she'd slept in it. She was carrying a battered cardboard suitcase, and, by God, nobody was going to steal that damn thing from her; she plunked it down on the floor so close that she could keep the toe of one of her patent leather shoes pressed firmly up against the side of it. The moment she sat down, she started talking. She had an accent pungent enough to strip the paint off the walls; I guessed it to be Tennessee or Kentucky or even downstate West Virginia. She was right on the edge of making her big break into the movies, she said. She'd been seeing agents, producers, directors. Everyone was enthusiastic. Tomorrow she'd probably get to take her first screen test. In the meantime, could I buy her something to eat?

"Sure," I said, "order what you want."

She ordered fries and a Coke, went on telling me about the agents and the producers and the directors. She was wearing a blue ribbon around her neck. It seemed an odd touch even for her thoroughly odd outfit. As she talked, she got more excited. She gestured; her head bobbed up and down. The ribbon slid out of place, and I saw that someone had once tried to cut her throat.

I could see that Revington liked that tale—probably even well enough to tell it as his own. "Los Angeles," he said, nodding, "yes, yes." We ordered another round.

He told me that his father had pulled strings to get him into WVU, that the moment he'd got to Morgantown, he'd rented a ratty little apartment just like mine and put up a huge sign over his desk: DON'T FUCK UP AGAIN. And he'd worked his ass off. "I thought when you heard I was down there, you'd come back," he said.

"I thought of it," I said, although I hadn't.

Ah, Morgantown—now that we'd both put the damned place behind us, it gleamed in our memories like a misty slate-grey Shangri-La. Ah, The Seventh Circle, cheeseburgers at Johnny's, floating around with Cohen in the old days, how crazy he was with his throwing knives and his cream sodas—and Marge Levine, did I keep in touch with her? "No," I said, "I don't keep in touch with anybody."

"Cohen went back to Harvard," he said.

"Yeah, he did," I said. "I was with him when he decided to do it."

He didn't come up with the obvious next line, so I supplied it for him: "I know. Everybody's in school but me."

"Had your physical yet?" ASK NOT, ETC.

"Yeah, in L.A. Oh, sweet Jesus, it was insane. They cranked hundreds of us through . . . God knows, maybe thousands . . . in

27

less than two hours. They checked our hearts by tapping us briefly with a stethoscope. Do you think I'm kidding? I'm not kidding. You know how they examined us for hemorrhoids? We stood in a circle, about fifty of us, with our pants down and the cheeks of our asses spread, while a doctor passed behind us at a dead run. Some jerk looked at my feet. 'No, no, no, they're not the least bit flat.' Christ, William, they're flat as pancakes. They wouldn't believe anything I told them about the asthma I'd had when I was a kid . . ."

"Did you have asthma when you were a kid?"

"No, not really . . . But anyhow, I'm 1-A and fit to serve."

"Congratulations. Now listen to me, you dumb fuck. Go straight back to WVU and register for the fall semester. And then notify your draft board. I'll even drive you down to Morgantown."

WE CLOSED down the bar. We returned to a night that had not become any cooler. We were hopelessly plastered by then, and I'd begun to think, Christ, what did I ever have against this guy? He's my best friend.

"Hey," he said, "let's go wake Cassy up."

The Markapolous house was dark, but we walked around to the backyard and found one lit window on the second floor. "Yep," I said, "she's still awake. I knew she would be."

"OK," he said, "boost me up onto the porch roof." He took off his loafers. I knelt down, and he climbed onto my shoulders. The first thing I did was dump him onto the grass. I lay there giggling. "Jesus," he said, "Come on, John, you can do better than that." We tried again. He hooked his arms over the roof. I never would have imagined Revington doing it, but now he was giggling too. "Steady, you son of a bitch, you'll break my head."

Then he was scrambling on up the roof, reaching with one long arm to scratch on the window screen.

Cassandra's voice: "Jesus fucking Christ, you madman! What are you doing?" She sounded delighted.

"What's it look like I'm doing?" Revington said. "I'm in the process of falling off your roof."

"Oh, John," she said, seeing me standing below, "are you there too?" Was she disappointed to see me?

She let us in. Barefoot, her eye makeup scrubbed away, wearing pink cotton pajamas, she looked like a young girl, but she was carrying the book she'd been reading, one finger in it to mark the place: Camus, *The Stranger*. "Still reading that stuff?" Revington asked her.

"It's better than watching television. Jesus, where have you guys been? God, are you drunk."

"Got anything to eat?" I said.

We settled down around the kitchen table, and I constructed a massive sandwich out of every kind of lunch meat they had in the fridge. I helped myself to some leftover potato salad and a glass of buttermilk. Revington popped a beer. "We should enjoy this while we can," he said. "Our last days of freedom . . ."

"Oh, fuck," Cassandra said. "What are you going to do, William, enlist?"

"It might be the thing to do . . . something honorable . . ."

"Honorable, my ass. But yeah, William, it just might be the thing for you to do. With your family connections, you'd ride out your four years behind a desk. And a good war record wouldn't hurt your political career any."

"Listen to that salty bitch, will you?" he said to me. "Look, Cass, we've got to grow up sometime. We've got to do something."

"Sure, yeah, we've got to do something. I've got three more years at Bennington to do."

Chomping away on my sandwich, sweating in the too-bright, too-yellow kitchen, I realized just how drunk I was: pissed to the hairline. Revington wasn't in any great shape either. "John's going back to WVU," he announced owlishly.

"Oh, yeah?" she said. "That plan will last for about a day."

He ignored her. "Look," he said to me, "if you could just hang in there and get through . . . if you could just get that goddamned degree . . . you could go to law school. Shit, with your grades, you could get in anywhere . . . even Harvard. You'd like the practice of law, I really think you would. Not law school. Nobody likes law school. But the *practice* of the law . . ."

"I hadn't thought of that," I said. I didn't have the remotest interest in the law. I despised the law. But I was drunk enough, feeling such camaraderie with Revington, that it seemed like an excellent idea. "Maybe . . ."

"We could go into practice together," said Revington. "We could do civil rights work . . ."

"Oh, my God," Cassandra said, "if you clowns want to do civil rights work, why don't you go down to Mississippi and register voters? You give me a pain in the ass, both of you. Civil rights work? Jesus. You're just going to be another crooked politician like all the rest of them," she said to Revington, "and if you're crooked enough you'll end up governor of the state"; and to me, "You'd last in law school about ten minutes. And you're not going to write the next *Gone With the Wind* either. If you write anything, it'll be ad copy for Eberhardts' so they can sell more clothes to people like my silly little sister . . . And me . . . I'll be pushing a baby carriage around some goddamned New England suburb."

I was angry at her; glancing at Revington, I saw that he was too.

But we had to laugh. She laughed with us. "We're all caught," she said as though telling us another joke. "We're inescapably middle-class, all fucking three of us. And we're goddamn well caught."

A look passed between Revington and me, the message: What does she know? What can she understand of us, of our sorrows (young Werthers that we were), this beautiful girl? Our companion, but always, at the crucial shearing point, apart. Nobody was going to draft her.

As we drove drunkenly home, as we floated maudlin and gurgling home, talking about practicing law together, talking about the old days, he took my hand (peculiar gesture, that handshake), said, *"Marcello . . . buonanotte."* I climbed out of the car, stumbled in to bed, saw by the thermometer on my mother's sewing table that it was eighty-seven degrees, by my clock that it was four in the morning. It was late enough, and I was drunk enough, to sleep.

I WOKE the next afternoon, deep-fried in my own sweat, thirsty enough to drink a lake, thinking: Law school! Jesus Christ, I must have been out of my mind. ASK NOT WHAT YOUR COUNTRY CAN DO FOR YOU. Revington had been right, of course: I *was* fucking up; I *was* drifting. For the first few months after I'd dropped out of WVU, the world had still seemed shot through with dazzling possibilities. Cohen and I had run on the beach; he'd taught me how to meditate. But then, at the end of the summer, he'd gone back to Harvard, and I'd stayed in Miami. Why? I still didn't have the answer. Over the years, Cohen seemed to have applied his motto "words are no damned good" even to writing letters; his messages had become more laconic, more infrequent (approaching, perhaps, the silence he'd always longed for); in a recent note, he'd said: "One thing appears to be certain: we're not going to be *young* saints." Saints? Hell, I would have settled for a reasonable facsimile of normal. Cohen had a girlfriend. I'd met her briefly, and liked her: a lean tall no-nonsense Cliffy who played field hockey and reminded me of Natalie. But I hadn't been within ten feet of a girl, hadn't even asked out the pretty teenage waitress who'd obviously been interested in me—that's back when I'd been lean, brown, and golden haired, and that, my friends, was a long time ago. What had I been doing? Nothing that I could see beyond generating four hundred pages of raw writing that was, I knew, still a hell of a long way from being publishable. Oh, this is intolerable, intolerable.

I'd been drinking so much that I'd long ago stopped having hangovers, merely arose aching and dull, needing Bromo, a pot of coffee, and, to settle my stomach, my usual breakfast of corn flakes and canned peaches swimming in heavy cream. Every day I'd ask my father how he was doing. He'd always answer, "Naw tah goo," which I'd learned to translate into, "Not too good." Nothing moved on the TV screen until evening when my mother turned it on for him, but he sat in front of it nonetheless, smoking cigarettes and watching its blank eye. One side of him remained paralyzed; he drooled occasionally down the rigid right side of his face. He'd been making a fair recovery; then, while I'd been in L.A., he'd had another stroke, a small one, but enough to blast away all but the last vestiges of speech. I sometimes wondered what he was thinking. Whatever it was, I'd never get to hear it. He did talk to me sometimes, but his words were thick, wet, and garbled. I was never absolutely certain I'd got the gist of them. All I could do with him was sit in front of the tube and watch reruns of Johnny Yuma. Strange to see him there: stopped: as if someone had driven a nail through a pocket watch.

While I'd been in L.A., my mother had sold our house. For years—while I'd been down at WVU, and then, later, while I'd been rambling pointlessly around the country—I'd always counted on that house, had always known it would be there waiting for me, everything in my bedroom exactly as I'd left it, but now we were living in a run-down apartment farther up Front Street and everything of mine was packed away in cartons and stored in a locker in the basement. There were only two bedrooms, one for each of my parents; when I'd arrived, my mother had moved into the front bedroom with my father, giving me her bedroom. I used her sewing table for a desk. When I paced up and down, smoking and trying to write, I couldn't avoid seeing myself, fat and bleary-eyed, looking back from the mirror on her dresser. The scent of her powder—lilac and violets—was everywhere. She'd stacked a little white bookcase with her Wedgwood bowls, her blue Fostoria glass, her porcelain figurines. During the heat wave, she kept fans going in every room, but not even a gale could have cooled that back bedroom. Out of a morbid desire to know exactly how bad things could get, I'd put a stand-up thermometer next to my typewriter; by the middle of the afternoon, it was usually registering over a hundred.

It wasn't just the house; she'd sold everything valuable, even her piano. She was working as a librarian's assistant, and I guessed that her piss-ass salary must have been most of our income (or even, God knows, all of it), but I didn't ask. She'd give me a few bucks from time to time—enough to buy beer and cigarettes—and when I thanked her for it, she'd always make a vague gesture of dismissal: "Oh, honey, I wish it was more." She'd come home from the library and cook dinner for the three of us (for me it was lunch and sometimes even breakfast); I helped her out by doing the shopping. She never told me to be careful with the money, but I pinched every penny. We ate spaghetti and macaroni, rice and beans, Salisbury steak and pork chops.

My mother seemed to think it was important that I "go through my things." She must have said that to me a dozen times. At first, I didn't understand why—those cartons buried in the basement locker weren't bothering anybody—but eventually I got it: going through your things is something you do before *you leave*. I'd dream up yarns about my future plans, making it all up as I went, look over and catch her tilting oddly away. It wasn't as though she didn't care. She'd always been, in some indefinable but crucial way, never quite at home for me, and now she seemed even more remote. She talked about the people she met at work; she talked about my father—and cried once: "Oh, John, it breaks my heart. He used to be such an immaculate man!"—but she never complained about herself. As I had my whole life, I tried to read her feelings from the vague clues she left floating in the air, elusive as butterflies. I never got the feeling that she was eager for me to leave, but she certainly didn't want me hanging around forever. I guessed that all she wanted was for me to do *something*, preferably (although not necessarily) somewhere else—that is, simply to take care of myself. I suppose I could have looked for a job, but if I had, it would have been an admission that I was going to stay in Raysburg for a while, and I had no intention of staying in Raysburg for a while. But I had nowhere else to go. *Oh, this is intolerable, intolerable.*

WHEN I emerged from bed late one Sunday afternoon, my mother said, "That little Markapolous girl called you." Maybe to my mother every female under twenty was still a little girl, but even so, that seemed a strange way to describe Cassandra. I called back, and Cassy said, "No, it wasn't me. Must have been little sister. Hang on a minute."

In an instant Zoë was effervescing at me: "Hi, John, are you doing anything today? Do you feel like taking some pictures? I've been waiting for it to cool off, but it's never going to cool off . . ." and on and on: her Courrèges copy dress, and some other outfits she'd put together, and some editorial shots she'd show me in *Seventeen*, and I was thinking, oh, right, for *her book*. "I don't even own a camera, Zoë." That was a lie; I still had my old Argus from high school.

"That's OK," she said, "Dad's got one. A really nice one. He said you could use it if you were careful. I bought film too."

As I walked toward Cassy's house, I was met by the bright whir of the lawnmower and the grotesque figure of Doctor Markapolous, his white hairy legs sticking out of plaid Bermudas, his pot gut hanging out: this funny cheerful man waving at me. "Hi there, John, how goes the Confederacy?"

"Oh, just great," I lied. "Twenty more pages."

"Fine, fine. And how are you doing?"

"Is that a professional question?"

He laughed. "God, you're a flip kid. No, just inquiring after your soul."

"My soul's wallowing in free-floating angst."

"It's called youth," he said as he began to manhandle the lawnmower through the thick grass. "Things that bother you in your twenties don't seem much of a problem in your fifties. And I know my saying it won't do you any good at all."

How the hell did he get so cheery? Maybe I should have gone into medicine.

I walked around to the back of the house and found Cassandra lying on a beach towel in Lolita sunglasses and a white bikini, a stack of books next to her. I couldn't understand how she did it; no matter how much beer she drank, she stayed as lean as ever. "Jesus, Cass," I said, "you look sexier than seventeen harem girls."

"Yeah? Well, what I am is braised like a short rib."

I sat down next to her on the towel. In the direct afternoon sun I began to sweat in torrents. "So where's little sister?"

"Preparing her outfits. Her costumes. Her goddamn wardrobe. Whatever models call it. Jesus."

Cassandra had rubbed every inch of her exposed body with baby oil, and plenty of her body was exposed. The white of her bikini flared out to an eye-blistering solarized nothingness against the gleaming surface of her skin; as brown as I'd got in Florida, she was browner. I could see nothing of her eyes; the surface of her sunglasses reflected back nothing but sky. She was, I thought, positively iconic. "Do we have to sit in the sun?" I asked her.

We moved to the front porch glider and drank iced tea with fresh mint. I closed my eyes to try to clear away the blaze of afterimages. "I was trying to remember," I said, "what color your bikini was . . . that time when I dropped by here and found you in the backyard."

"You mean when you first met me?"

"Yeah."

"It was blue. Turquoise blue. Dad had a fit when he saw it. I wasn't allowed to wear it to the pool, and it wasn't even that brief."

"It was pretty brief for those days."

She'd taken her sunglasses off, but I still couldn't read her face. "I'll never forget the first time I tried to talk to you," I said. "It was right here. On this glider. You were sitting exactly like that . . . with your feet up on the railing."

"What's this, nostalgia time?"

No, I thought, just trying to connect with you. "Something like that," I said, "*Déjà vu* maybe. I remember admiring your ankle bones . . ."

"Oh, God," with a laugh.

"Boy, was that hard. Everything that came out of my mouth just sounded unbelievably stupid."

"Hard? You think it was hard for you?"

We swung gently. It had never occurred to me that it might have been hard for her too. "I didn't care what you said," she told me. "You could have said anything. I knew perfectly well you'd come to see me."

"Yeah? How'd you know that?"

"Oh, for Christ's sake, you had it written all over you. And then you made me wait damn near two months before you came back again, you son of a bitch." Her voice had been flat as a breadboard, but she was smiling slightly. I felt a silvery shiver down the back of my neck. "Oh, come on, Cassy," I said, "you seemed so cool."

"Yeah, I was cool all right . . . I was just out of the eighth grade, and you'd already graduated from high school."

Amazing. In the five years we'd known each other, we'd never talked about any of this. "Did you think you were too young?"

"Oh, hell, no. That never crossed my mind. I had a highly inflated opinion of myself . . . except for my figure. I didn't think I had much of a figure. But I certainly thought I was mature enough for you . . . Oh, I knew I'd get in trouble with Mom, and I did. And it took me a long time to believe you were serious, and . . . Well, I couldn't pretend to be . . . I even knew it at the time . . . I remember thinking he better like me for who I am, because who I am is who I am."

"That's wonderful," I said. "That's exactly how you came across."

"Oh, yeah? What a pain in the ass I was. I can't believe myself sometimes. I remember thinking that I was so much more complicated and interesting than all those . . ."

With a bang of the screen door, Zoë was out on the porch with us. Her hair was up on rollers. "Cassy, why didn't you tell me John was here?" and then to me: "Do you want to see Dad's camera? It has a whole bunch of lenses with it . . ." She was raining words down on us like handfuls of bright beads. "Wish we had a studio . . . the backyard over by the hedge . . . in the living room maybe . . . a real romantic prom look . . ."

"Zo," Cassandra said, her voice uninflected and deliberate, "can you leave us alone for a minute?"

Little sister stopped in mid-flight. "But John's said he'd . . ."

"I know what John said. John will come and play with you in a minute, all right?"

Zoë's emotion was compressed into a single blue-eyed flash. She wasn't miffed or annoyed or even badly deflated; she was genuinely hurt. Then she turned and was gone, letting the screen door slam behind her. I felt a pang of sympathy for her. "The light's not right," I called after her. "The sun's still too high."

"Oh, for fuck's sake." Cassandra collapsed back onto the glider, let her head fall back so she was staring upward at the ceiling. "How the hell did you get so goddamned fat?"

"Jesus! Why does everybody keep asking me that? I drank a

38

lot of beer. I ate a lot of crap. I sat on my ass and wrote half a fucking book."

She didn't say anything. "There's no place to walk in Los Angeles," I said, feeling monumentally sorry for myself. Oh, this is intolerable, intolerable. And then another wave of fury struck me like a mugger having a second go. "How the hell did you get so *bitter?*" I yelled at her.

"Give me a cigarette."

I offered her the pack. She hesitated, then pushed it away. I followed the direction of her eyes. Her father still had two or three passes to make over the lawn; he'd paused to mop his forehead with his handkerchief. "I can't take another goddamned lecture," she said. "I don't *care* what's happening to my cilia. I don't *care* what's happening to my bronchia."

We watched her father finish up the lawn and push the mower into the garage. He walked into the house, and I handed her the cigarettes. "I don't know what's wrong with me," she said. "I wish the hell I did . . . Sometimes I think Bennington was a mistake."

"Yeah?"

"I probably should have gone to Antioch or Oberlin."

"What's wrong with Bennington?"

"Shit, it's not that bad. It's a good school. It's certainly liberal . . . It's just . . . The whole goddamn place is full of girls."

I laughed. She gave me a bleak smile. "Yeah, I suppose it is funny . . . Oh, fuck, John, I'm one of these weird girls who never had girl friends. When I was a kid, I was always one of the boys . . . and then you came along . . . and then there were always more boys coming along."

She shrugged. "Girls can be so fucking petty . . . Oh, some of them are nice enough. They're not all preppy New England

39

snots . . . although a lot of them are. And you know what *I* am? I'm 'the Greek girl from West Virginia.' That's great, isn't it? I don't even remember my grandfather . . . but when it turns out that I'm not an expert on stuffed grape leaves and the Parthenon, they don't know what to make of me. And *West Virginia?* They don't even know where it is, for Christ's sake. I didn't know I *had* a West Virginia accent, but I guess I do. Jesus."

Now she was inviting me to laugh with her, and I did. "Oh, it's not that bad," she said, "or . . . you know, unbearable or anything like that. Like Camus says, in the long run you get used to anything. But whatever I do, it's never quite right. It's not a big blatant thing. It's really subtle. I can't quite put my finger on it. But I just don't . . ."

"If you're different," I said, "they pick you to pieces, but if you try to be like them, that doesn't work either because they know you don't mean it."

I could see I'd surprised her. "Christ, you've got a good memory," she said after a moment. "You're the only person I know who can quote me back to myself."

"Well, it is kind of similar, isn't it?"

"Of course it is. But I don't *want* my life to be Canden High School over and over again forever . . . just an endless series of places where I've got to figure out how to fit in. Shit, maybe it gets easier. Maybe I should let Zoë cut bangs in my hair so I'd look like Françoise Hardy. I don't know. Maybe William's right. Maybe it's just growing up."

"But not like he's doing it. Can't you see how hard he's working at it?"

"Oh, yeah. But maybe that's what it comes down to in the end. Like Sartre says, you choose yourself. But what he doesn't say is that you've got to choose from what's possible."

"Do you really think you're going to end up in some New England suburb pushing a baby carriage?"

"I just said that to piss you guys off. But yeah, that's probably what will happen to me."

That wonderful turn of phrase from *The Port Huron Statement* popped into my head. I hadn't thought of it for years. "So the message you're getting," I said to her, "is that there's no viable alternative to the present?"

"That's good. That's it exactly."

"But there's got to be a way out, Cassy."

"Yeah? Where is it?"

MY WAY out was my Civil War novel. It was my secret ace in the hole, my only consolation. I'd called it *The Rest Is Silence* (I'd thought that a perfect title for a story told entirely from a Confederate point of view, one that ended in crushing defeat and the bleak hopeless days of Reconstruction), and all I had to do was finish my first draft, read the manuscript over again and tighten it up, send it around until I found an enthusiastic editor (my Maxwell Perkins, an infinitely patient guy with impeccable taste who would help me impose some order on the damned thing), and then it would be published, shoot to the top of *The New York Times* best seller list, and I'd be off to the races. Not being a complete idiot, I knew that it probably wasn't going to be quite as easy as all that, but I did believe in my own talent. I kept telling myself that if I worked on it every day, eventually I'd get somewhere— maybe not exactly where I thought I was going but certainly farther along than I was at the moment.

I had slipped into the novel sideways, merely amusing myself in the Void, certainly not setting out to do anything as arduous as writing a book. I'd always wondered about my great-grandfather, the first John Henry Dupre. Had he really been from New Orleans? Had he really ridden with Morgan? Who the hell was Morgan? If Morgan had not been a phantom fabricated by my father, if he'd actually existed and fought in the Civil War, then his career must be on public record. One weekend soon after I'd arrived in L.A., a weekend in which I was bored beyond belief and nearly dying of loneliness, I went to the public library and looked him up, discovered within ten minutes that Morgan had not only been a real person but had been famous—or notorious, depending on which side of the war one's sympathies lay.

His name was John Hunt Morgan. His mother's family, the Hunts, were Southern aristocrats; his grandfather, John Wesley Hunt, was the first millionaire west of the Alleghenies. Morgan was born in Alabama in 1825 but raised in Lexington, Kentucky. (Ah-ha, I thought, that's where my grandfather died, so there's got to be a connection.) Morgan had a university education and, by all accounts, was the walking personification of the Southern gentleman: hot-blooded, headstrong, independent, and honorable. He grew up in the Kentucky of the grand manner, of blue-blooded gentry living side by side with wild frontiersmen, of fox hunts and grand balls, of duels fought at dawn over a lady's honor. He served in the Mexican war, saw action at Buena Vista, returned to Kentucky, founded the Lexington Rifles in 1857. He advocated the secession of his state, joined the Confederate forces as soon as the war began, commanded the 2nd Kentucky Cavalry— "Morgan's own." He became a colonel in 1862 and, later in the same year, was promoted to brigadier general.

A dashing, smiling officer with a debonair mustache, six feet tall, immaculately dressed even in the most harrowing of circumstances, John Hunt Morgan drew legend to himself like lightning to a rod. From the mythologizing of the heroes of the first

American Revolution (Confederates called theirs the second), from Arthurian legends and the example of the English cavaliers, from Tennyson and Scott and the popular romances of the day, the South had developed an ideal of what a soldier should be—a Christian warrior, a gallant knight—and what is most amazing is not that such an antique model of behavior should have been pitted against the practicality of the Yankee war machine, but that so many of the Confederate generals, headed by the saintly Robert E. Lee, managed to live up to it.

Southerners idealized John Hunt Morgan, called him "The Thunderbolt of the Confederacy," compared him to Robin Hood. In the North, he was a ghostly, terrifying figure called "Morgan the raider." His cavalry could outride any Yankee on horseback, and Morgan had the nasty habit of turning up hundreds of miles from where anyone thought it was possible he could be, often well to the rear of Federal lines. A military court of inquiry once asked a Union major, apparently in all seriousness, if he had any evidence that Morgan had ever been seen in two places at the same time.

In July of 1863, Morgan, exceeding his orders, made his most famous raid—through Kentucky, Indiana, and across Ohio nearly to the Pennsylvania border—one of the longest rides by regular cavalry behind enemy lines in the history of modern warfare. For twenty-five days Morgan tied up nearly all the Federal forces in the Midwest; it's estimated that 110,000 men were looking for him before it was over. Trading spent horses for fresh as he went, Morgan used up 15,000 mounts, took his men over a mountain that locals claimed could only be climbed by goats, destroyed ten million dollars' worth of Federal property. He was captured at the point farthest north ever reached by an armed Confederate force, was sent, not to a military prison, but to the

Ohio state penitentiary at Columbus. He pulled off a storybook jailbreak—some historians believe the stories current at the time that he tunneled his way out, others claim that Confederate agents bribed prison officials—but, despite a massive manhunt, he managed to escape back to the South.

Morgan, who was always the master of the grand gesture, once gave a captured train as a token to the local Yankee ladies. His critics suggested that it might have been more to the point if he'd burned it. His raids were the very stuff of high romance, but he disobeyed orders, did what he damned well pleased. Confederate generals grumbled that he'd be more useful as the regular cavalry extension of Bragg's army than as an unpredictable independent raider galloping through the North.

Accounts of his last days make sorry reading. It's as though Morgan had begun the war thinking of himself as Parsifal but ended it realizing he was Don Quixote. The cream of Southern chivalry was dead by then; many of the men who filled Morgan's last command were little more than bandits. He couldn't control them. Looting had become epidemic. Morgan was about to be relieved of his command. His friends say that a profound gloom settled over him, that he knew he'd never live to see the end of the war. The Yankees, he said, would never make the mistake of capturing him alive a second time. His death was mysterious. Some say he was betrayed by a woman, others that he was done in by his own stupidity. The Michigan cavalry who took him appeared to know exactly what they were doing, rode directly to the house where he was sleeping. He was shot down in a grape arbor. The entire South mourned.

So that was Morgan. Honorable, daring, independent. Rash, insubordinate, stupid. The perfect metaphor for the South: a gentleman and a jackass. And wasn't it a fabulous story—a perfect story for a ten-pound novel and then, later, for a spectacular treatment on the big screen? You're damned right it was, and I really wanted to tell that story.

FOR SEVERAL nights after I got off work (I'd landed the job in the camera store by then), I paced up and down Sunset Boulevard mulling it all over, trying to figure out the best way to go about it. I decided that I needed an observer, someone off to the side, involved in the action but not at the center of it—someone to play Nick Carraway to Morgan's Jay Gatsby—and I soon had that character. He was a quiet watchful fellow with a shadowy background. He was said to have fled New Orleans after killing a man in a knife fight, or maybe it was a gun fight, no one knew for sure. I called him Henri Leblanc. He wasn't a big man (was about my height, as a matter of fact); he spoke with a slight French accent, was always impeccably dressed, and made his living as a gambler.

As the story opens, Leblanc has just escaped, in a flurry of gunplay, from a riverboat where he was accused of cheating at cards. He hides out in the mountain fastness of Western Virginia, down in Hatfield and McCoy territory (where I had never been and about which I knew nothing). There he is befriended by a wild mountain clan of pig farmers and moonshiners. The patriarch of the clan has a beautiful young red-haired granddaughter who falls in love with Leblanc. Her name is Evergrace; in several touching scenes, she sings Elizabethan ballads and accompanies herself on the dulcimer. Although he's moved by the beauty of the place and the rude dignity of the folk (and, of course, is charmed by Evergrace), Leblanc knows that he can't settle down in the mountains. One night there's a drunken fight. Up until then, Leblanc has gone out of his way to avoid trouble, but his patience has worn thin; he whips out his hidden Bowie knife and throws it into the heart of an obnoxious lout. Then, at dawn, he gallops off to Kentucky to join the Confederate Army.

Hearing that the great Morgan needs men in his cavalry, Leblanc rides to Lexington (where I had never been and about which I knew nothing) where he meets the dashing ne'er-do-well blue-blood, Fraser MacGillivray, who is serving under Morgan. Leblanc and MacGillivray become instant friends, and MacGillivray introduces Leblanc to the best families in Lexington, including the Tubervilles where, at a grand ball, Leblanc meets their youngest daughter, Eleanor, and falls in love with her at first sight . . . And that's as far as I'd gone with it. The war hadn't started yet, Morgan was still offstage, and I'd already covered four hundred pages. I was, I thought from time to time, probably doing something wrong. Maybe there was too much detail. Maybe I should have opened the story in Kentucky, not Western Virginia (although that didn't feel right somehow). But one thing was certain: it wasn't going to get finished if I didn't work on it.

In one of the dozen or so how-to-be-a-writer books I'd consulted in L.A., I'd found a bit of advice that had made perfect sense to me: never revise until you have a completed first draft. So day after day I'd forced myself to plow ahead without ever looking back any farther than yesterday's work; that's the way I'd piled up those four hundred pages. A year and a half of my life had gone into those pages, and I still hadn't read them straight through from beginning to end.

AFTER DINNER we retired to little sister's territory. It was slightly cooler down there, almost pleasant, with shafts of sunlight through the high slit windows lighting up the brilliant colors of Zoë's fabrics, with a rotating fan gently riffling through the pages of her fashion magazines. Sonny and Cher, on the radio, were proclaiming their eternal love for each other while, on the old tattered couch, Cassandra was taking the rollers out of Zoë's hair and throwing them into a shoebox. "My God," she said to me, "do you remember when I used to set my hair every damn day? Boy, am I glad I don't have to do that anymore."

"You *never* had to," Zoë said primly. "You have naturally curly hair."

I was studying the good doctor's camera; of course it would be a Nikon. I replaced the standard 50 mm. lens with the 80 mm. portrait lens, looked through it. What I'd always told prospective buyers was absolutely true: Nikons did have the loveliest focusing system in the world. I zeroed in on the cornea of Zoë's right eye; the lens put me practically in her lap. "Miss Fairfax wants me to try a lot of different looks," Zoë was saying. "She says you've got to be versatile . . ."

"Who's Miss Fairfax?" I said.

"The old bag who keeps taking Dad's money," Cassandra said.

"She's not an old bag," Zoë said, annoyed. "She's the head of *the agency*."

"Oh, we've got a modeling agency in Raysburg, do we?" I said. "And *Miss Fairfax?* Christ, nobody in Raysburg, West Virginia, is named Miss Fairfax."

"Her name was probably Myrtle Gotz," Cassy said.

"Will you guys stop making fun of me?" Zoë said. "You can hurt my feelings, you know."

Zoë must have been planning her photo shoot for days. She had everything worked out in a notebook—at least a dozen different looks. She'd sketched each one with cartoon drawings that I thought were genuinely clever; in a precise, unbelievably tiny handwriting she'd listed every article of clothing she would need all the way down to her underwear. Paper-clipped to her notes were pages torn from magazines so we could see exactly what she wanted. "For Christ's sake, Zo," her sister said, "we're never going to get through all these."

"Oh, sure we will. They're all with the same hairstyle . . . except for the last one . . . well, sort of the same."

"God, this is worse than playing dress-up when you were six."

"How would you know? You never played with me."

"Touché," I said.

"I'm not kidding," Zoë said to me. "When we were little, Cassy thought she was a boy."

"No," Cassandra said, laughing, "I always knew I was a girl. That was the trouble."

Big sister and I went outside to scout a location while Zoë ran up to her bedroom to create her first look. I stood Cassandra in a deep blue afternoon shadow and took light readings from her face. The low sun was blasting through holes in the hedge; I could use it as a back light, but I'd have to be careful. "If I didn't know you," Cassy said, "I could almost believe you knew what you were doing," then, as she saw her sister trotting out from the house, "*Gloves*, Zoë?"

In spite of the heat, Zoë was wearing not only shortie gloves but a nubby wool jumper with white ribbed stockings, on her feet deft little ghillies that looked fresh from the box. She was carrying a purse that matched the shoes. "It's a back-to-school look," she said. "You see a lot of this in *Seventeen*." I looked at her though the lens. As I'd guessed it would be, the light was exquisite; against the deeply absorptive green of the hedge, her skin seemed to glow with an inner radiance. I focused on her impossibly blue eyes. "You look fresh as a dewdrop," I said.

"God, Dupre," Cassandra said, "you're such a poet . . . Hey,

48

did you get a load of the bow? Turn around, Zo."

Zoë spun on her heels to show us the back of her head; her hair was caught back in a blue bow that must have been a foot across. "Back to school?" Cassandra said. "I'd just love to see you turn up at Canden High looking like that."

"This isn't for real, dopey. I'm a girl in a magazine."

"Oh, is that who you are? I was afraid for a minute you were you."

"I wanted to do one really prissy look . . . you know, all scrubbed and polished . . . everything matching . . . one hundred percent the lady."

"One hundred percent the lady? One hundred percent the candy-ass is more like it."

Zoë made a small strangled yelp that I realized was a giggle. She covered her mouth but couldn't stop. "Don't do that, *dopey*," her sister said. "You'll get lipstick on your pretty white gloves."

"Stop it, stop it, stop it!" Zoë was laughing so hard she was bent forward, holding her sides.

"Oh, dear God," Cassandra said to me, "where did that pathetic thing come from? Somebody please drown it in the bathtub."

"Come on, Cassy," Zoë gasped out between spasms of laughter, "that's not fair." She didn't look much like a model, but the giddy girl I was watching through the lens might be, I thought, cute enough to be preserved on film, so I started to shoot.

"OK," Cassandra said, "I'll be good . . . Take a couple deep breaths. You can do it, sweetheart. You look terrific, no lie . . . OK, now *sell us those damn clothes.*"

Zoë turned her back on us. When she faced us again, I could see how hard she was concentrating. "OK," she said and began posing, imitating the girls in *Seventeen*. She'd obviously learned a thing or two from her Mickey Mouse modeling courses, and soon

I could see what she was trying to do, even anticipate her. At first she looked stiff, but gradually something magical began to happen; she was no longer riding on her innate beauty but reaching for something deeper. "Hey, she's pretty good," her sister said.

"You're damned right I am," Zoë said, and her eyes fired a stinging bolt of blue electricity straight down the lens. I caught it. I was getting better too.

WITH CASSANDRA egging us on, I shot Zoë in polka dots and stripes, in paisley and lace, in voile and cotton, in rayon and wool; I shot her looking schoolgirlish, looking demure, looking Romantic, looking Young London, with and without bows in her hair, in a kerchief and a little cap that Zoë called a "helmet" (but Cassandra called a "baby bonnet"), in knee socks and loafers, in nylons and pumps, in her Courrèges copy dress and go-go boots. Now Cassandra and I were sitting in the dining room, waiting for little sister to come back and present us with what she'd sworn would be her final image.

Looking through a camera lens had made me keenly aware of light. The low golden blaze of the late afternoon sun was transforming even the most commonplace objects—the oak table, the silver candelabra, the marble top of the antique sideboard, the crystal in its display case, the threadbare Oriental rug on the floor—into objects of rare beauty. The light was perfect. "What's taking her?" I said.

"Oh, this one's a major production."

The sharp nose-twisting smell of nail polish remover sprang into the room: Cassandra was changing her white polish. "Zo's got the right idea," she said. "If you're a girl, you sell your looks. Nobody really gives a shit about anything else."

I hadn't realized before how exhausting it was to take pictures.

I could feel a thick weariness settling onto me. "One of the girls at school," Cassandra said, "Sandy . . . Her older sister graduated from Bennington with an honors degree in history, and guess what she's doing now? She's a Playboy Bunny."

I laughed.

"Yeah, it is funny," Cassandra said, "but do you know what she makes? Two hundred and fifty fucking bucks a week. She said it's not too bad. Like being a cocktail waitress in a Halloween costume. And the customers aren't allowed to ask you out. They're not allowed to touch you," and she paused to give the proper ballast to her punchline, "not even your tail."

"Oh, great."

"The horrible thing is I keep thinking about it. I could do it for a year, save my money, and go to Europe."

"Oh, come on. You're not serious, are you?"

"Sure I'm serious. Where else could I make that kind of money?"

I couldn't imagine anyone more ill-suited to being a Playboy Bunny than Cassandra. I found the very thought of it repellent. It was almost as bad as if I'd announced that I was going to join the Marines. "Jesus, Cass," I said, "that's ridiculous."

"It's not that ridiculous. What the hell am I going to do with an English degree from Bennington? Be somebody's secretary? Get married? The only thing I can think of I might want to do . . . the only thing that's *possible* . . . is go to New York and try to get on as a junior editor in a publishing house or something like that . . . along with a million other smart-ass girls with degrees who have exactly the same idea."

Cassandra hadn't yet changed into her evening uniform, was still wearing her white bikini, but with a boy's shirt over it. She sat sideways in a massive wing-back chair, her bare legs draped over one of its arms. The golden light pouring through the open window burnished her deeply tanned skin. She looked impossibly alive—far too alive to be talking about what was or wasn't possible. The last of her nails painted, she screwed the brush back into the polish bottle (careful, careful, don't smudge a nail), waved her hands in the air. Smiled at me.

We heard Zoë's distressed voice wailing from upstairs: "Cassy! Please come help me."

"Oh, no," Cassandra said. "*Cassy, puhleeze.* God, that's funny."

"Hurry her up," I said.

Cassandra left me alone. I thought of getting a beer, but that particular light, I knew, would be as brief as a suspended teardrop and I didn't want to miss any of it. I could hear the high-pitched timbre of Zoë's voice, her sister's lower soothing tone. The good doctor and his wife were talking too, a distant murmur. Outside, the lawn sprinkler was swishing and a single bird was hitting the same note repeatedly, a sharp sound like a nail on metal—*chip, chip*—that seemed a punctuation to the only thing I could make out from the intoning voice of the TV: *Vietnam, Vietnam, Vietnam.* I felt as though something truly significant was about to happen, and then I realized that I would never be there again, exactly as I was, exactly at that moment—smelling the newly cut grass and Cassandra's nail polish remover and her father's aromatic tobacco and something else. What? Cassandra didn't wear perfume; she'd never worn perfume. Could it be the flowers outside?

She crossed the room quietly and sat down again in the antique chair. "Well, is she coming?" I said.

"Almost. She hasn't quite achieved perfection yet. She's wearing my prom dress. Jesus, all the effort . . ."

"Cass," I said, "you aren't really thinking about being a Playboy Bunny, are you?"

The question stopped her for a moment. "Oh, come on, Dupre, I know you. You'd love to see me in a Bunny costume."

"Fuck, Cass, you wouldn't last a night. You'd piss off all the customers."

"No, I wouldn't. For two hundred and fifty bucks a week, I'd be the dumbest bunny you ever saw."

"Oh, for Christ's sake. You'd hate it."

"Yeah, but so what? In the long run, you get used to anything, right? Unlike you and William, I operate in the realm of the possible."

"But what if the possible's intolerable?"

She didn't answer, but she'd just admitted me to the inside of her head, and it was every bit as bleak in there as it was in mine. I'd always depended upon her for . . . I wasn't sure what: a fierceness, a clarity, the untamed spirit of the back-alley tomboy she used to be. In the old days, she would never have talked about operating in the realm of the possible. If this was growing up, I didn't want her to grow up. "Cassandra," I said, "remember when you drove down to Morgantown with Cohen? And you and I watched the dawn from the top of North High Street?"

"Of course I do. Did you think I'd forget?"

"I don't know. That was a long time ago."

There was no mask now, and not a even a hint of a smile. She was looking directly into my eyes. She could have been sixteen again. "I didn't forget," she said. I'd just got what I'd wanted ever since I'd come home, and I felt the impact of it shiver through my body all the way down to my toenails. "OK, Cass," I said, "we're linked. We were linked then, and we're still linked . . . Here's the deal. If one of us gets out, then the other one's got to do it too."

Now she did smile. "You mean it, don't you?"

We heard Zoë's heels on the stairs. "Yeah, I do," I said. "Shake on it?"

"God," she said, "you're such a fucking Romantic," but offered me her hand. I took it and held it.

"I'm really sorry," Zoë said. "I didn't know it would take so long." She crossed the few feet of the Oriental and turned to face us. I could read her uncertainty from the way she moved—shyly, almost diffidently. "It doesn't work, does it?" she said.

The prom gown was a timeless blue taffeta with a full skirt that was shorter on Zoë than it would have been on Cassy, but not quite short enough—as though it couldn't make up its mind whether it wanted to be the length called "ballerina" or the one called "princess." Zoë was wearing little white flats, crochet stockings and gloves; she'd brushed her hair up in the back and rolled it, leaving the long bangs in the front, and those touches were certainly *now*, exactly what you'd see in *Seventeen*, but she'd done her makeup like an adult model in *Vogue*—probably only trying out what they'd taught her in modeling school—and it was far too much. Her exposed neck and shoulders looked clean, young, and fragile, but the face she'd created was—and no other simile would do—as artificial as a doll's. "Don't worry," I said, "It'll make a great photograph," not sure that it would. "Sit where Cassandra's sitting."

Zoë smiled at me gratefully, and the sisters traded places. Zoë gathered her skirt under her and settled into the wing-back chair. I looked through the lens. "The sidelight on your stockings is terrific," I said.

Cassandra began to fuss with her sister's hair, hiding some wisps at the back of her neck. "Oh, my God, the prom," she said to me. "I can't believe I ever went to it. It feels like somebody else's life."

I took a light reading. We'd missed the golden moment; all that was left was the long last slow blue fade. I'd have to shoot wide open. I'd have no depth of field at all. "I'm sorry, you guys," Zoë said.

"Oh, shut up, little sister," Cassandra said softly, "you're so pretty."

I DIDN'T know how Cassandra and I had ended up on the back porch in the dark; it was where we used to go to be alone when we'd first met, but that was a billion years ago when the earth was still cooling. We'd watched the last of the smoky twilight drift away into full-blown night; there was no reason why we should be, but we were speaking in hushed voices. "You know," she was saying, "it's almost a curse to be born with her looks. And she's . . . Well, she's not dumb. She's anything but dumb. She just seems awfully young sometimes. She's a lot younger than I was at her age."

"Yeah," I said, and put verbal quotations marks of irony around the phrase: "but you were 'wise beyond your years.'"

"Oh, yeah. Sure I was. But she seems . . . I don't know . . . pre-conscious."

Pre-conscious? Where had she learned that one? First-year psych? "I wouldn't be too sure of that," I said. "Did you look at the notes she made? She seems fully conscious to me."

"Come on, she doesn't have a clue what she's playing around with." Then with a wicked teasing inflection: "Does she get to you?"

"Fuck off, Cass," but I was thinking: *You* get to me.

"Oh, I know," she said, "it isn't just you. She'd get to anything male. Christ, I'm glad I was never like that. And you know what's funny? It's all sublimated. As soon as she discovers the joys of boys in cars, this modeling crap will go straight down the tube."

Inexplicably annoyed, I said, "I don't think so. It doesn't have anything to do with sex . . . Well, that's not true. It's got everything to do with sex, but it's got so much to do with sex that it flips around and reverses itself . . . so it isn't about sex at all. Does that make any sense?"

There was just enough light so that I could see her expression; she was smiling. "No."

I wasn't sure what I'd meant, but I knew I was onto something. Then, apropos of nothing—or maybe apropos of everything—she said, "William made a pass at me."

I gave her my most noncommittal interrogative monosyllable: "Ah?" William Revington, I thought, you son of a bitch.

"Yeah, he did. Earlier in the summer. Before you came back. I couldn't believe it. He's engaged to that little moron from Charleston, so what does that make me? A free piece of tail?"

"I wouldn't take it too seriously. I think he regards it as his manly duty to make a pass at anything female."

"But *me?* Jesus, he's known me since I was ten. You'd think the incest taboo would kick in or some damn thing . . . Oh, it wasn't a big dramatic number. It was one of those things you could take as a joke. But I knew he meant it. Part of me was flattered and another part of me wanted to knee him in the balls. Remember all the shit he gave you when you started taking me out?"

"Oh, yeah. You know what he said? 'Isn't that cherry a little bit green for you, John?'"

"Christ," with a laugh, "the vermin. You know, I'd like to go to bed with him once just to see if he could do it."

After a while the silence began to pile up around us like some idiot's mile-high construction of fragile dishware. She hadn't really meant anything by that, I told myself. It had just been another of her smart-ass remarks—so what I should do was find a good Raymond Chandler wisecrack that would move things along, something wry and astringently funny, but all I had in my head was an appropriate verse from the Bible: "For he that hath, to him shall be given, and he that that hath not, from him shall be taken," but then, perfectly timed to save us, Zoë stepped out from the kitchen. "Do you guys want to be alone?"

"No," Cassandra and I said simultaneously. "It's OK," Cassy said. "Come on out, Zo," I said.

Zoë sank onto the top of the steps leading down into the garden. "Oh, that was so much fun." She'd changed into shorts and a halter top, but she hadn't taken off her elaborate makeup. In the faint light that was left, her face looked entirely unnatural and eerily beautiful; transformed by the Purkinje Shift, her lips burned as darkly as the roses at the edge of the lawn.

I lit two cigarettes, passed one to Cassandra, listened to the desiccated churr of the locusts. The back porch was depressing; why the fuck were we out there? I'd had too much to drink, and there were too goddamn many memories out on that back porch. I said to Zoë: "Your sister's been telling me how she's going to be a Playboy Bunny when she grows up."

"Oh?" puzzled. Then: "I can never tell when you guys are kidding."

"That's OK," Cassandra said. "We can't either."

DAYS PASSED, a thousand combat infantry landed at Camranh Bay, Dean Rusk told the North Vietnamese that they'd better watch out or we'd bomb their asses off, the Marines creamed the Vietcong near Da Nang, Johnson was thinking about calling up the reserves, the heat wave did not break, it did not rain, and I did not work on my novel. I usually avoided weighing myself, but one morning in July, driven by morbid curiosity, I stepped onto the bathroom scales and discovered that, just as I had suspected, I had been growing inexorably larger. For the first time in my life I was over two hundred pounds. My God, I thought, I have become gigantic. Later, flipping through my Civil War books, I discovered that on that very weekend in 1863, everybody in Raysburg had been expecting John Hunt Morgan to drop in. I took it for an omen.

Morgan had been in the midst of his great raid—on the run by that time, desperately trying to find some place to cross the Ohio, escape his pursuers, and vanish into the mountains of West Virginia. He'd already made one attempt—at Blennerhassett's Island down below Parkersburg—where some three hundred of his men did manage to get across before a Federal gunboat appeared. Had Morgan attempted to cross up the river here at Raysburg, he would have been met by Brigadier General James S. Wheat with a sizeable chunk of the West Virginia Militia, but the Thunderbolt of the Confederacy knew better and was already miles north in rural Ohio, riding hard. The folks here didn't know that, however; terror swept the town: "Morgan's coming! Morgan's coming!" Church bells were rung, horses hidden in the woods. Every male with a gun had it cleaned and ready. And people sat up all night waiting for those apocalyptic horsemen who never arrived.

I called Revington to tell him all about it. "Christ, man," he said, "you've hit two hundred pounds on the very same day when Raysburg was *not* invaded? I can't believe it! This calls for a celebration. You know what we need, Dupre? Mint julep."

I called Cassandra. "You're so full of shit," she said. "Come on over, I'm boring myself to death."

I didn't know how to make mint julep, so I settled for a fifth of J. T. S. Brown, drove out to Cassy's house. She was reading Camus on the front porch glider. "What the hell you got there, Dupre?"

"Some of that old J. T. S. Brown. Want a snort?"

"That's a very evocative name . . ."

"Yeah, it's Fast Eddy's drink in *The Hustler*."

She laughed. "Oh, Jesus. You guys are incredible. So what are you playing today, Jackie Gleason?"

"I'm gigantic."

"Yeah, you sure are. You keep on going, you're going to look just like the sheriff of Ohio County. No . . . no, I don't want any of that damned stuff. I've still got some pride, you know. At least I can wait till the sun sets."

Within minutes Revington drove up, parked, and strolled toward us carrying a gallon milk jar. "Excuse me, son," he said to me, "do you know the road to Morgantown?"

"No," I said happily, taking up an imaginary guitar, "but if you hum a few bars, maybe I can play it for you."

"Oh, for Christ's sake," Cassandra said, "you guys really are pathetic."

He set the jar down at my feet. "It should be a demijohn, but I couldn't find one."

"All right, I'll be the straight man," Cassandra said. "Excuse me, William, what's that?"

"Aren't we celebrating John's gigantism and Morgan's raid? It's mint julep." He picked up the jar with both hands, raised it, and saluted me with it. Ice cubes tinkled. "To your health, sir," he said, "and to a steady increase in your weight. May you achieve the stature you so richly deserve. And to the South, sir. Long may she simmer."

"Amen," I said. "You know, it really is the perfect metaphor . . . Morgan's raid. Raysburg on this very day," and I allowed myself to expand to the mellifluous oratorical tones of a Senator Phogbound, "as is the inevitable destiny of this hallowed city . . . as it will be its destiny forever . . . was once again bypassed . . . by anything important." I took up the jar and drank. "Yow, that's got a bite to it."

"Do you clowns want glasses?" Cassandra said.

"No, no, straight from the jar," I said and passed it to Revington.

"It's like Kierkegaard's rotation method," she said. "It may not be much, but it's all we've got. Every night we can change drinks."

"The hot water at ten," Revington muttered in a deeply funereal voice, "and if it rains, the closed car at four . . ."

"But of course it's never going to rain," I said. He offered me the jar; I took it and had another good gulp. I could, I thought, develop a taste for this damned stuff. "Stetson!" I yelled, "how the hell you been, man? I haven't seen you since the war."

"I'm doing just fine," he said. "I read much of the night and go south in the winter."

"You guys are just so unbelievably full of shit," Cassandra said. "Oh Jesus, another month and my sentence is up."

The light was changing, the shadows cooling toward blue. The violet hour, I thought, still drifting along with Eliot, and it was enough, for the moment, to be sitting there getting plastered with my friends, talking nonsense, the taste of mint and bourbon in my mouth, with no plans and no need of plans. "Hey," Revington announced. "I got a call from Alicia." Ah-Lee-Sha. "She's back in the States. She's in New York."

"How nice," Cassandra said, "and how is the darling little girl? Did she have herself a peachy-keen time in Paris?"

Revington's face shifted. His grin fell away, his jaw tightened and his eyes looked away, focused somewhere between the houses across the street; it signaled a change of persona as clearly as if he'd laid down one mask and picked up another. "I probably shouldn't be," he said quietly, "but I'm worried about her."

"Oh, what did she do," Cassandra asked, "get a run in her stocking?"

He sent an angry glance at Cassy, opened his mouth to say something—didn't say it. His face closed; he looked into my eyes, invoking our bond against her. "What's the matter?" I asked him.

"It's complicated. She really misses me . . . I miss her too, of course, but . . . Well, she wants me to fly up to New York and surprise everybody. She thinks if I just appear, it'll be OK. But I know her mother. It would really piss her off . . . I mean, tactically we could get away with it, but strategically it's not the greatest idea in the world . . ."

"Oh, yeah," Cassandra said. "You can't piss off Mom. You're not just marrying sweet little Lissy, you're marrying her whole goddamn family."

Revington looked at Cassandra a moment, his eyes narrowed as though assessing her. Then he turned to me: "Listen to that salty bitch, will you? What are we going to do with her?"

"Who says there's anything you *can* do with me?"

"So Alicia wants you to come up anyway?" I said, trying to move the conversation along. "How long's she going to be in New York?"

"Oh, just a week. We can wait a week, for God's sake. I tried to explain it to her, but . . . Well, your brain can be telling you one thing, but when your heart tells you . . ."

"Oh, come on, William," Cassandra said evenly, "do your duty like a man. Fly on up there and put the horny little girl out of her misery."

I saw that Revington had not simply adopted another pose; he was genuinely angry. Oh, great, I thought, so much for the violet hour. I was trying to think of something soothing to say when, from inside the house, Mrs. Markapolous called: "Cassandra."

"Oh God, now what? . . . Yes, Mom?" and then she was gone, letting the screen door slam behind her.

"That goddamned arrogant little bitch," Revington said, smashing a match into fire. "How does she get off with being such a fucking little bitch? What she needs is a good, thorough, methodical, therapeutic screwing. Jesus Christ, I swear I'm going to nail that high-assed little bitch."

"No, you won't," I said.

"You want to bet?"

"Sure."

"A bottle of Scotch."

"Sure."

"You're on, Dupre. I'll fuck her before the summer's over." I extended my hand, and he slapped it, grinning. Now why the hell did I do that?

Bang! back through the screen door, Cassandra: "My mother is too polite to tell you gentlemen, but she is afraid that we are not presenting the proper image to the neighborhood. It just will not do for us to be sitting on the front porch drinking whiskey out of a milk jar. She wonders if perhaps you gentlemen would not feel more comfortable on the back porch."

THE NIGHT is closing around us like the screwing-down of the aperture on the good doctor's Nikon; mosquitoes have begun to needle my forearms. I am sitting with my shoulders against the back porch railing; my shirt is glued to me; I can feel sweat trickling down my sides. And I'm watching Cassandra loll about in the crook of Revington's arm. Oh, this is intolerable, intolerable. The son of a bitch had started to make his move, and Cassandra had not been at all one of Diana's elusive does, had rather come to him like a bridled mare. He's talking on, his voice pitched with

62

resonant sincerity, invoking himself in power—politics. He'd worked for Johnson in sixty-four; he'd met some of the top Democrats in the Northern Panhandle. And now he knows all those damned old-time crooked Democrats in Alicia's family down in Charleston. He's presenting us with snapshots of meetings behind closed doors, in back rooms, those famous back rooms where decisions are made *in camera*, far from the sweating populace. He's telling us how Kennedy bought West Virginia. "It's not just about spending money," he's saying. "It's an art . . . like being a great actor. They talk about the Kennedy charisma as though it didn't take any work. But no one realizes how much planning goes into it. Care. Skill. Timing." The image before the lenses; get it right for the lenses. Presenting himself now to Cassandra: look at me, I am potent. *Potens, potentia.* I'M A LONG TALL TEXAN. Oh, Jesus, this is intolerable.

I wander into the house. Zoë's in the living room with her boyfriend—a tall quiet kid—and with another couple. Zoë must have decided that her Courrèges copy wasn't just for her book after all; she's wearing it, and she looks spectacular. The good doctor is having himself a drop of Scotch; he's discoursing to the boys on Vietnam. I stumble up to the bathroom. I'm dragging my bottle of bourbon along with me, absent-mindedly. Most of it has gone into the julep jar by now, but a couple good shots left. I drain the bottle and step on the scales. Dressed, I weigh two hundred and seven pounds. I lie down in the dry bathtub, tilt back the bottle, and lick up the last drop of bourbon. I am boiled, I am plastered, I am drunk as seven skunks. What am I doing here? ASK NOT, ETC. Intolerable. Perhaps I'll take a nap in the bathtub. Someone's banging on the door. "Hey, John, you've been in there forever. What are you doing?" Zoë.

"Damned if I know." I climb out of the bathtub; I find move-

63

ment surprisingly difficult. "Sorry," Zoë says when I open the door, "but other people have to get in here too, you know."

"I'm gigantic," I say idiotically. Her hair is curled, her eyelashes are curled, and she's painted her lips and fingernails pink. It's just as hot as it's been every other damn night since I've come back to Raysburg, but she's wearing stockings—and her go-go boots of course. I've photographed her in that dress, so I've certainly had a good look at it, but I still can't believe how short the skirt is. I put my arms around her, murmur, "Ah, Zoë, are you one of Lyndon's little majorettes?"

"Oh, good grief," she says, laughing at me. "Come on, John, cut it out. Stop it, you're drunk."

"No shit."

"Hey, let go." Giggling, she slaps my wrist so hard it stings. "Cut it out. I mean it."

"Ah, Zoë, my love . . ."

"You're really being silly." She's pushing me. "Out, out, out. I'll have an affair with you when I'm twenty. Now just get out of here, OK? That's it, just keep moving forward. Out, out, out."

I'm floating down the stairs, carrying my empty bottle of J. T. S. Brown with me. The whole house seems to be rocking gently, as though we've drifted away down the river. Passing the living room, I wave languidly to the good doctor, ooze through the kitchen and out onto the back porch. "The problem that Johnson faced in Congress . . ." Revington is saying. Oh, Jesus. I sink down onto the floor next to the julep jar. The ice has melted long ago, now just tepid mint-flavored whiskey. I've got my muzzle sunk into it, gulping away. Revington's shirt is open; Cassandra is playing with the hair on his chest. In the dark, her white fingernails stand out starkly against his skin. I RIDE FROM TEXAS ON A BIG WHITE HORSE.

"Mah fellow Ah-mericans," I yell, imitating Johnson's shit-kicker accent. "I know I told you'll I was a *peace* candidate. That, howevah, was just to get my sorry ass elected. Now I'm gonna bomb the fuck out of those little bastards . . . Jesus Christ, Revington, I *voted* for that hypocritical peckerwood. Now I wish the hell I'd voted for Goldwater."

There is a silence in which I can imagine Revington regrouping. I am, I know perfectly well, not precisely welcome at that moment on that back porch. "Yes, that's just the sort of man for you, Dupre," Revington says, "a loser like Barry Goldwater. The biggest piece of political flotsam in recent American history."

"An honest man," I say, "stupid and wrong, but honest. The last of a vanishing breed. From now on, only the most wretchedly empty of men will go into politics."

Revington doesn't answer. It's too dark for me to see his face. And all that mint julep is running through me like water through a sluice gate. Christ, I can't climb those stairs again. I jack myself to my feet, lean against the side of the house, and begin to piss off the porch. The sound of the urine splashing onto the lawn is somehow very appealing. "What the fuck are you doing, Dupre?" Revington is yelling at me.

"What the fuck's it look like I'm doing?"

He stands up, drags Cassandra by the hand toward the door. She pulls free of him. They stand there a moment—two silhouettes against the light from the kitchen. Then he shrugs and goes in. She hesitates, then follows. "Do you think you're going to get rid of me that easily?" I'm mumbling. I follow. Revington has closed the door. As I reach for the knob, I hear it lock.

I begin to chuckle, take off at a run, around the house, up the steps. Revington has beaten me to the front door. It's locking just as I jerk open the screen. I'm suddenly furious. "You goddamn prick, I'll kick your teeth down your throat," I yell at him. Through the small window I see him blow me a kiss and turn away.

I wander to the back porch and the whiskey jar. My blood is pounding in my temples; a red haze is beginning to float in front of my eyes. Some detached part of me is saying, "It's not just an expression. You really do see red." And then the detached voice is gone, and I'm smashing the back door, ramming my shoulder into it. "You can't keep me out," I'm yelling. "I'm gigantic."

The wood is cracking. I'm immensely satisfied with the sound of it. CRACK. SMASH. Revington is just inside. I can see him. He's leaning against the door. He's afraid of me. Good. I hit it again. CRACK. Inside the house are running footsteps, voices, yelling. The front door bangs. Footsteps running around the house. I look down; at the bottom of the stairs is Zoë, giggling at me. "John. What the hell are you doing? You're breaking our door."

With a whoop, I leap off the porch directly at her. I land on all fours in the grass, and she's running away, laughing. "Zoë, my love," I yell. "Light of my life! Fire of my loins!" And I've leapt up and am running too, chasing her.

She's screaming with laughter. I'm howling and barking like a dog. At a dead sprint we've run around to the front of the house and I'm chasing her up the street. Her little white go-go boots are flickering in the dark just ahead of me.

PAIN. The world has tilted on me. I'm flat on my face on the pavement. I roll over onto my back. "Owww, owww, owww!" My God, that's my voice. I'm baying like a whipped beagle. I've run into a fireplug.

Cassandra is looking down at me. "Stop it," she gasps out between spasms of laughter, "you're fucking pathetic."

"Owww, owww, owww!"

"Stop it, John, you'll have the neighbors out."

And here's Zoë, panting and giggling, staring down at me. "John? Are you all right?"

"Owww, owww, owww!" I pull up my pants leg, feel my shinbone. It's still in one piece, thank God, but my hand comes away bloody. "Owww, owww, owww!"

"For God's sake, please stop it." Cassandra's caught up to us. She's laughing so hard she sinks to her knees on the pavement.

Zoë looks genuinely concerned. "Come on, Cass, let's get him up," she says. They lever me to my feet. There's a sister under each of my arms. "Come on, help us, John. Don't just hang there. You weigh a ton."

"I'm gigantic."

"No shit. Come on, walk."

I begin to shamble toward the house. And here, hesitantly, comes Revington to meet us. "You miserable prick," I yell at him. "Save your Confederate money, Revington, the South's going to rise again! Ho Chi Minh forever! Juan Bosch Presidente! Hang Lyndon Johnson from a sour apple tree!"

I was too drunk to drive home; Revington had to take me. As I was getting out of his car, I said, "I'm sorry, William."

"You asshole," he said.

I DREAMED that I had caught up with Zoë. I grabbed her by one of her white go-go boots and spilled her down onto the grass in front of me; she flowed down in slow motion, like honey out of a jar. I lifted her little skirt, found the smooth semi-ovals of her bum, and then, in my dream, I did what I'd never done before, not even in my imagination—entered her as easily as sliding my hand into a warm, moistly oiled glove. I woke up. My hangover was appalling. I lay, naked, flat on my back on my steam-bath bed. My mother was standing in the doorway, looking at the far wall. I was topped with an erection as obvious as the Washington Monument. "You should cover yourself, John," she said. I rolled onto my side and pulled a sheet over myself.

"It's nearly one in the afternoon," she said.

"Yeah, Mom, I'm getting up soon. I've been contemplating it."

"That little Markapolous girl called you. She's called you twice."

"Which one? Cassandra?"

"No, the *other* one. The *little* one." I could hear the disapproval in her voice. "What did you do to your leg?"

"I ran into a fireplug."

"A fireplug?"

"Yeah. I was running down the street and I ran into a fireplug."

Her face pursed; she seemed to be on the point of saying something. But she didn't say it; she lingered a moment and then began to back out of my room, closing the door behind her. "Hey, Mom," I said, "I'm thinking of going back down to WVU."

She stopped. "WVU?"

"Yeah, you know, Mother, it's the state university they have down there in Morgantown."

"Oh, John," she said, annoyed, "don't be like that."

"If I stay here I'm going to get drafted." ASK NOT, ETC. I hadn't intended to yell at her, but I was yelling.

"Oh," she said. I began to suspect that she was going to leave, simply, without saying a word. Her face seemed pinched, drawn forward to a point; the point hung there, unsure which way to go. Finally she said, "You're going back to school?"

"Yeah, I guess so . . . anyhow I'm thinking about it."

"Oh, good Lord . . . Well, I suppose I can always go back to Household Finance."

I gulped down a Bromo, sat with my father in front of the blank TV screen, drinking coffee and smoking. "John?" he said. It was one of his words I could always understand, although it came out something like "Zhuh."

"Yeah, Dad?"

"Drin smush?"

What the hell was *drin smush?* "What's that, Dad?" I leaned closer to him.

The side of his face that worked was attempting a grin. "Dju drin t-t-t-tuhsss smush?"

"You're goddamn right I drank too much." I touched my forehead to illustrate.

He made the harsh coughing sound that I'd decided a while back was a laugh. He lit another cigarette and so did I. "John?"

"Yeah, Dad?"

"Wunna t-t-t-talia . . ."

I leaned closer. A burst of spitty unintelligible syllables came out of him. "Sorry, Dad, I'm not getting it."

The good side of his face was twitching. He seemed upset. "Shih," he said, which I translated into "shit." Then he made another run at it. All I got was something that sounded like "mahoe gawnduh fise." Could that be "my whole goddamn face"? But what if it wasn't? Oh, this is intolerable, intolerable. "Do you want more coffee?" I said.

"No. Juswanna t-t-t-talia," and then try to tell me he did, but I couldn't make out a word of it.

"Wait a minute. I'll get Mom."

He made a pushing gesture with his good hand. Sometimes he could be clear as a bell: "Piss on it."

I walked into the kitchen and regarded the phone as though it were a sleeping copperhead. What in God's name could I possibly say to Zoë? Some kind of apology was obviously in order. But what if she didn't answer? What could I possibly say to *her mother?*

Zoë answered on the third ring. "Oh, John, how are you? Are you OK?"

"I'm fine. A little hung over."

"I bet you are. How's your leg?"

"It hurts, but it's OK . . . Zo?"

"Yeah?"

"I'm sorry I pawed you in the bathroom and chased you up the street. I mean I'm deeply, profoundly, and genuinely sorry."

"That's OK," she said, giggling. "I just thought it was funny . . . until you ran into the fire plug. Boy, were you drunk. I've never in my life seen anybody that drunk. You were a riot."

That was me all right, a full-scale riot. From where I was standing, I could see the wrecked figure in front of the silent TV set. After two strokes the asshole was still smoking, and I was sure that if somebody poured it for him, he'd still be drinking too. The horrible thing was that I'd always rather liked him drunk. With most of a bottle of rye in him, he'd been a talkative fool, a joker, an affectionate slob who'd pat me like a dog, a man who would (as I'd seen with my own eyes) dance around a party with a lampshade on his head. Now I seemed to be following firmly in his footsteps, and last night had been the pinnacle of my success—my finest performance to date as a fat drunken buffoon.

I heard Zoë sigh. "Are you ever going to get my pictures?"

I'd been meaning to do it for days—another thing I'd fucked up. "Sorry, Zo. They're still at Middleton's. I'll get them first thing in the morning, I promise . . . Hey, is your sister there?"

"No, she's not here right now. You broke our door, you know."

"I did?"

"Yeah. Not just the hinges. You cracked the wood right down

the center. I'm not sure I should say this, but . . ."

"What? Go ahead and say it."

"Dad's going to have to get the whole thing replaced. He says he should send you a bill, but he doesn't really mean it. He says he's always considered you a member of the family. But Mom's really mad. She's madder than hell. She's madder about you relieving yourself off the back porch than she is about the door . . . and she's plenty mad about the door."

"Great," I said.

"John?"

"Yeah?"

"Do you want me to tell you what to do?"

"Sure. Tell me."

"It'd help a lot if you told her you were sorry. You know what I mean. And do it today. And get her some flowers. She'd really like that. Roses. She likes *yellow* roses."

I HAD to take a cab to Meadowland to get my mother's car, and then I had to drive to Ohio to find the yellow roses. "Why, John, are these for me? How nice."

"Mrs. Markapolous . . . I'm sorry about last night."

"Yes, John, I imagine you are."

"Look, I'm really sorry about your door. Maybe I could buy you a new one?"

"Oh no, John, you don't have to do that. I'm sure nothing like that will ever happen again."

"No, of course it won't . . . there's not even the faintest possibility . . ."

"John." I jumped a foot. The good doctor. I was still so deeply lost in the trackless waste of my hangover that I hadn't heard him coming. "I want to talk to you."

71

I followed him into his study. He shut the door, sat at his desk, lit his pipe. I sat in the chair in front of the desk. I wondered if he was regarding me as a patient. "I prepared a little speech," I said.

"I'm sure you did."

"Do you want to hear it?"

"Of course. I've always been a sucker for prepared speeches."

"Look, Dr. Markapolous, I'm sorry I got hopelessly plastered and pissed off your back porch and broke your back door and chased your daughter up the street. I'll never do anything like that again."

"How's your leg?"

"It hurts like hell."

"Pull up your pants."

He cleaned off the dried blood and put a bandage over my shinbone. I thought it was nice of him. He sat down again behind his desk. "John, I know you're under a lot of stress."

"What do you want to do, refer me to a psychiatrist?"

"Hell, no, I don't want to refer you to a psychiatrist. Most of the ones I know don't have the brains of a sardine. When somebody has a problem, there's usually a simple solution. You're worried about getting drafted aren't you?"

"Yes."

"What are you going to do about it?"

"I was thinking of going back to WVU."

"Great. That's the most sensible thing I've heard out of you all summer. Any problem going back? How are your grades?"

"My grades are just terrific."

"Well, get right on it, John. Get your student deferment back. You're running out of time. If you don't get moving, you'll end up in the army by default."

"I know."

"It's a damn stupid ridiculous war and you don't want any part of it."

"You bet."

"I approve one hundred percent. Go back to school. Stay out of this war. They have enough cannon fodder. Work to change things." He stood up. "Have I been talking through my hat?"

"No," I said, "of course not. You never talk through your hat . . . Look, do you want me to pay for a new door?"

"Christ, no, I do not want you to pay for a new door." He put his hand on my shoulder. "You're welcome in this house any time, John," he said, "just do your heavy drinking somewhere else, OK?"

I didn't know what to do next. I hadn't seen Cassandra anywhere. I could go back home, but almost anything in the world was better than going back home. I settled onto the front porch glider, my head pounding. I lay back and closed my eyes. Why did it have to be so goddamned hot? I heard the screen door open and close; I felt the motion as Zoë sat down next to me. "Mom really liked the roses. She said it was very thoughtful of you. She asked me to ask you if you want to stay for dinner."

"That's nice. Tell her I'd be delighted. Where's your sister?"

Zoë didn't answer. I sat up, opened my eyes, and found her looking at me. I didn't have a clue what was going on, but I knew that something was. She held my gaze a moment, then looked away. "She's at the country club," she said.

"The country club?" It didn't make any sense.

"Yeah, William took her to the country club. She even put a dress on. I haven't seen her in a dress all summer."

IF MRS. Markapolous had stopped to consider the implications of it, she probably wouldn't have asked me to stay; if I'd had a brain in my head, I wouldn't have accepted. It was classic summer night's food—ham and potato salad. We filled our plates at the kitchen counter, carried them to the table, sat down, and regarded each other. Then we must all have been thinking much the same thing: *My God, this is awkward.* Cassandra was gone, leaving behind her a black hole the size of a galaxy, and I was left with Zoë—and, as both of her parents knew perfectly well, I was the very same fellow who, only the night before, had, like a demented fool in a bad farce, been barking like a dog while merrily chasing Zoë up the street. "John tells me he's going back to WVU in the fall," the doctor announced in an insistently cheerful voice.

"What a good idea," his wife beamed at me. "You were so close to getting your degree, it'd be a shame not to finish."

"Yeah," I said, "a year and a half. I could even do it in a year if I went to summer school."

"Cool," Zoë said.

Now I'd just said to them what I'd said to my mother—sending her, God help me, back to Household Finance—but was it possible that I could really *do it?* And instantly my mind conjured up an image of myself hermetically sealed into some ratty little basement apartment in Morgantown, sitting up all night trying to bang out a paper on Wordsworth. But no, it wouldn't be Wordsworth. I'd already done the Romantics. Maybe it'd be Webster or Kyd. Now wouldn't that be fun? Revington had told me that Morgantown's tiny chapter of SDS had died when Marge Levine had left, and times had changed. In the age of the Beatles, there probably wasn't any room left for an authentic ethnic folk singer—even if I could have revived that venerable role. So how about the serious young novelist? Would that impress freshman girls? But no, more than likely what they would get was the fat drunken buffoon. Oh, this is intolerable, intolerable.

We slogged our way through dinner, and then the good doctor said, "Well, John, how about a game of chess?" So that's what I'm doing here, I thought. I haven't been left with Zoë after all. I'm *a member of the family*. "Sure," I said.

The doctor and I had always been fairly evenly matched—although, on a good night, I could usually take him—but I hadn't played chess for years. I drew white and confronted him with my Russian closed front, which, as it was meant to, baffled him into an excess of caution and led us into a maze of complexity and tedium. I was having trouble concentrating. I never played chess without remembering the night when Natalie had showed me, for three games in a row, what a real chess player looked like, and, thinking of her, I felt a wave of that old dangerously bittersweet longing I'd been trying like hell to avoid; back in my university days, it would have caused me to write a poem.

Oddly for such a grown-up tomboy, Natalie had worn a lot of perfume—a bright splashy girlish scent—and I suspected that if I were ever to smell it again, I would weep like Pagliaccio. On my list of the most disastrous mistakes of my life, letting Natalie go was very near the top. It wasn't as though she'd been the love of my life. If anyone fit that bill, it was Cassandra, but, at that very moment, Cassandra, the love of my life, wearing a dress for the first time that summer, was dining at the country club, probably sitting on the terrace watching all the lovely rich children cavort in the pool, accompanied by my oldest friend, the lean and sexy William Goddamn Revington, whose avowed and entirely malevolent intention was to screw her ass off. Oh, this is intolerable, intolerable . . . But anyhow, back to Natalie. Most people did not end up marrying the loves of their lives, and Natalie and I had been happy with each other, and maybe even could have married each other, but then again, maybe I was just wallowing in my old familiar hog trough of nostalgia—the most perfect girl was always the one who got away—and right now *any* girl would look good, and the doctor was making his next move, exactly the one I'd been expecting. I advanced my queen's bishop to say, "Watch it buddy, not so fast." But at the top of the list, the height of my stupidity, the most ghastly mistake I'd ever made had been dropping out of WVU. If I hadn't done that, I'd have a BA and I'd be off to grad school in the fall to study some damn thing at some damn school or other, and my draft board could kiss my ass.

Had I really let Carol Rabinowitz fuck up my life? After that hideous last encounter with her, I should have walked around Morgantown for a few hours, gone back to my apartment and got a good night's sleep, gone back to classes, and then started attending the meat-market mixers at the Lair until I found myself a pretty wholesome freshman girl who would have been duly impressed by older and worldly-wise me. But that isn't what I'd done. Well, the light in the tropics had been exquisite, and something in me must have needed to soak the sun into myself until I was hot to the bone, and it wasn't as though I'd never thought of any of this before. Over the years I'd chewed it all to a sour indigestible pulp. "Check," Doctor Markapolous said.

Shit, I thought, how did that happen? I stared at the board and saw that my convoluted Russian game was unraveling from every corner. I had to protect my king, and the minute I did, there would go that exposed pawn—zip—and then what? I didn't have the energy to work it out. I resigned. "Are you sure?" the good doctor said. "There's many a slip . . ."

"Yeah, I'm done. You've got me good."

"Care for another?"

"No, thanks," I said. "I can't think straight tonight."

I bade the good doctor a good night and stepped out onto the front porch. I was far from sleepy, and the Yacht Club was closed on Sundays, and there was nowhere else I was going. (Hey, I thought, that's just like the Dylan song.) I had most of a six-pack left at home, so it could be cold beer and my fashion mags, or even watching TV with my wrecked father. But I couldn't move.

Zoë stepped outside, closed the screen door quietly, and sat down next to me. "Hi," she said as though she'd just met me on a street corner.

"Hi," I said. Out of nowhere, a bit of Rilke appeared in my mind: *Ach, die Gärten bist du . . . ach, ich sah sie mit solcher Hoffnung.*

We swung together for a while. She'd settled into a posture— back perfectly straight and knees together—that was almost prim. Maybe that's how you sat next to an unpredictable lunatic: carefully. "What are you thinking?" she asked me.

I wasn't thinking of anything, damn it; I was sinking further into melancholy. The lines had been from one of Rilke's short, unbearably sad poems I'd memorized when I'd been at WVU, and, if I wanted to abandon myself to a one-way trip to the bottom of the pit, all I would have to do was recite it to myself word for word. It was strange to have Rilke sneaking up on me again. I hadn't thought about him in years, but I used to hear his German sounding even in my dreams. If I'd been talking to Cassandra, I would have explained all of this to her in far too much detail—God, what a boring pretentious asshole I could be at times—but, because it was Zoë, I said simply, "I was thinking about German poetry."

She gave me an inscrutable sideways look. "I don't think that's what you were thinking about."

"Oh, yeah? What do you think I was thinking about?"

She didn't answer for a moment. Then she said, "She doesn't really like him. She was just bored."

I was too stung and startled to do anything but snap back at her: "She may not like him all that much, but she thinks he's sexy."

"*I* don't think he's sexy. I think he's a jerk."

I looked at her. She was looking out at the empty street. Her profile was as exquisite as a cameo. Maybe she *could* be a model. And I didn't want to be discussing big sister with little sister—I couldn't imagine anything more impolitic—and I certainly couldn't talk seriously about any of the twists and turns of my untrustworthy mind, but I couldn't just stand up and leave either. "Well, Zo," I said in the hearty voice of an adult addressing a six-year-old, "was that your boyfriend who was here last night?"

"Who? Jeff? . . . Oh, he's taken me out a few times, but he isn't really my boyfriend . . . not yet anyway."

"Do you want him to be?"

"I don't know . . . I think so. Maybe. I like him, but he's . . . I don't know. Shy. He's going to be a senior."

"And what are you going to be? A sophomore?"

"No, a junior." She sounded annoyed.

"Two more years, huh?"

"Yeah. What a drag."

She sighed. We swung on the glider. Then, with no preamble, she hit me with a deluge of words: "Miss Fairfax says if I was in New York, I could be working right now . . . Oh, she understands how important it is to finish high school. She always says I should finish high school. But I talked to Dad . . . I *tried* to talk to him, and . . . He always said we could talk about anything, and then when I tried to talk about it . . . I said maybe I could go to New York and find a nice family to board with and finish high school there, and then I could see if I could really . . . but I guess he didn't really mean it. I guess there must be some things you can't talk about . . . I mean, all I wanted to do was *talk* about it . . . He just got mad at me. He's never got that mad at me before. He *yelled* at me. He called me 'a little hare-brained idiot.' Well, I'm not as smart as Cassandra, but I'm not a little hare-brained idiot."

"No, you're not. Of course you're not."

"He wants me to go out to Brooke. Or down to WVU. Would I like it at WVU?"

"No, you'd hate it. The girls down there think the height of fashion is the sweater set."

She giggled. "That's what I thought. Not everybody has to go to college, do they?"

"No."

This was not the Zoë I knew—or thought I knew. She had fallen silent. We sat there swinging, and I was getting more and more uncomfortable. "I think I better go home soon," I said. "I don't want to be here when Cassandra gets back."

"Oh," she said—a single round sad monosyllable—and, for only a second or two, let one of her hands rest lightly on the top of one of mine.

"Good night, Zoë," I said.

III.

FOR THE next few nights I stayed away from Cassandra's house. If Revington had won his bottle of Scotch, I didn't want to know about it. Instead I went to the Yacht Club on the Island. There was not a yacht to be seen, only a motley collection of noisy Ohio River speedboats, but that was OK with me; I'd always loved the place ever since my father had taken me there once to celebrate something or other, God knows what. He'd never needed much of an excuse to celebrate.

I'd been a year or two below the drinking age, but because I was with him, nobody asked me for my draft card. He ordered two beers at a time and gave one to me, and the bartender saw it and didn't give a shit, so I got pleasantly soused drinking what the old man drank: Miller's High Life. I'll always remember that night. It was crowded, a Saturday probably, but there didn't seem to be a soul my father didn't know (a lot of the guys called him by his old nickname, "Jiggs"), and I followed him from table to table as he shouted out greetings, slapped his pals on the back, pumped their hands, and shoved me forward into their grinning faces: "This is my boy, Johnny the Fourth." It was the first time I'd ever got drunk with him out in public, and I was proud that he was proud enough of me to want to show me off to fifty other drunks, and it was the first bar I'd ever seen that spilled outdoors along the river-bank. I'd thought it wonderful, bordering on miraculous, that you could get loaded by the river, and I still thought so—but now, unlike my father, I knew hardly anyone and had no inclination to get to know anyone. I sat alone at the farthest table and drank boil-ermakers. It was a perfect place for me (dirty and dimly lighted, I thought wryly), a place where nobody would bother me, where I could drink in peace. The lights of town were, as always, reflected and blurred in the black water. The moist, rank, muddy river smell, as always, told me I was home. Not much ever changed in Raysburg from one year to the next. I could imagine myself growing old in this town, sitting in exactly the same spot year after year, drinking exactly the same illegal bar whiskey and weak West Virginia beer, staring at the same river and wondering what the fuck it all meant. That is, of course, unless I got my ass shot off in Vietnam. ASK NOT WHAT YOUR COUNTRY, ETC.

What I'd learned in Morgantown was that hell was getting stuck inside your own mind; since then, I'd been trying to follow the advice of that great American sage, James Thurber: *Let your mind alone!* But coming back to Raysburg was not letting my mind alone, and now I was being revisited by an old familiar sorrow that was like a lame mangy dog who follows you home and flops down quietly in the corner, expecting nothing. I should never have come back, I told myself for the millionth time. I had every reason to be depressed, I told myself—the heat wave, my poor sad mother going bravely off every morning to her pissy job (not to mention Household Finance), my wreck of a father drooling in the living room, and, of course, Cassandra. She and I might very well be linked; she might remember what had happened at the top of North High Street and believe in it just as much as I did, but that didn't make us lovers any more than it ever had. I certainly didn't have a claim on her—at any rate, not in the ordinary way a boy makes a claim on a girl—and whether or not she slept with William Revington should have absolutely nothing to do with me, but, unfortunately, it did. Dumb asshole that I was, I'd even egged him on. "To everything there is a season," I kept hearing on the radio (Ecclesiastes, via Pete Seeger, via the Byrds), and the season for Cassandra and me was obviously long over: *"Wer jetzt allein ist, wird es lange bleiben . . ."* and with that, I was back in my ratty apartment in Morgantown, remembering, far too vividly, the pictures I'd taped to my walls. Oh, dear God, all the hours I'd spent staring at those pictures, trying to put myself inside them, melt into them. What on earth had I been doing photographing Zoë? Letting your mind alone requires a certain amount of distance, but it was impossible to maintain much of a distance through a portrait lens.

I was taking my drinking slow but steady. I knew myself well enough by now to be able to time it practically down to the last possible minute when I would order the last possible double that would nail it all home so I could wobble back up Front Street in a spinny summer night's blur to collapse, with nothing seriously left of me, into muddy sleep. Out in the river, carried along on the deep fast channel out in the middle of the river, a speedboat was drifting by with its engine cut. It was strangely lit with a string of pink and green and golden lights that looked for all the world like Japanese lanterns. I heard laughter drift across the water, and a strain of music, a British band, I thought (Zoë would surely know the group), and what seemed to be the voices of children calling to each other. I felt an inner shiver, then, in memory, heard a little girl's voice—"Ally, ally, out's in free!"—one of my playmates from when I'd been six or seven, maybe Cindy Douglas, in the pressing summer's twilight just minutes before I'd be called home to bed. Walking home later, I would pass the house where I grew up (now occupied by strangers) and Cindy's house where we'd played dolls and dress-up. I could turn at the bridge and, within minutes, walk over to Nancy Clark's house on Maryland Street, and it was all just too damned much. These fragments. Wearing Cindy's patent leather shoes, dreaming of wearing Zoë's dress, photographing Zoë, being photographed, not imitating a little girl but being one, looking up to see Nancy Clark as a princess (gold crown, blue dress, and petticoats), bright red lipstick, her face entirely unnatural and eerily beautiful, at the end of the Purkinje Shift her lips burning darkly as roses: "Come on, Alice, sit by me."

Maybe I *should* have been a girl. It was an annoying thought, an unproductive thought—a thought as utterly useless as wishing I looked like Gregory Peck—but it was not a new thought. If I were a girl, I wouldn't have to worry about getting drafted, but that seemed entirely beside the point. What kind of girl would I have been? A normal happy well-adjusted girl? Somehow I didn't think so. I imagined that I would have been just as much of an outsider as Cassandra, trying out one role after another, choosing from what was *possible* and never feeling authentically at home anywhere—in short, that I would have been much the way I was at the moment. Then, with a sensation like falling down an inner mineshaft, I saw that the fragments in my mind had made a pattern: if I could have been a girl, Zoë was the girl I would have wanted to be. The instant I arrived at that formulation, I went skittering away from it like a wobbling top.

But be that as it may, I told myself, in the meantime, while you are laying around Raysburg playing the fat drunken buffoon—longing for Cassandra as you have ever since you've met her, obscurely tantalizing yourself by taking pictures of her beautiful little sister, brooding about the past and musing upon it all in your usual poetic but utterly ineffectual way—your draft board could lower the boom on you at any moment. OK, GET UP TOMORROW BRIGHT AND EARLY AND DRIVE DOWN TO MORGANTOWN AND REGISTER FOR THE FALL SEMESTER. Yeah, I could do that, but somehow going back to Morgantown seemed almost as bad as getting drafted. WRITE A LETTER TO YOUR DRAFT BOARD, A CONFESSION SO

MAD THEY'LL KNOW JUST WHAT A RAVING LUNATIC THEY'RE DEALING WITH. TELL THEM YOU LIED AT YOUR PHYSICAL, THAT YOU REALLY DO HAVE YELLOW FEVER, JAUNDICE, AND ACUTE ANEMIA. WHILE YOU'RE AT IT, TELL THEM THAT YOU SUFFER FROM NIGHTMARES, WALK IN YOUR SLEEP, WET THE BED, AND SLEEP WITH BOYS EVERY CHANCE YOU GET. Hey, that's a good suggestion. I'll certainly keep that in mind. GET UP TOMORROW MORNING AND WORK ON YOUR NOVEL. THAT'S THE ONLY THING THAT COUNTS.

I GOT up the next morning and didn't work on my novel, and I didn't work on it the morning after that and the morning after that. I began to dread the mornings. I always drank too much at the Yacht Club, and I always woke up feeling like hell, and I'd fallen into the routine of pulling myself back together by having a cup of coffee and a smoke with my father. I was pretty sure he'd come to expect it, maybe even look forward to it, and every day, if I sat there long enough, he'd try to talk to me. He'd fix me with his good eye (the other one, although it worked, seemed as lifeless as a marble) and say, "John! Ahjuswanna t-t-t-talia."

"Yeah, Dad," I'd say and lean closer to him.

Whatever it was he wanted to tell me, I just couldn't get it. Spitty mysterious bursts of syllables would come splattering out of him, and I could usually understand a word or two, but as to deciphering it, reading French Symbolist poetry would have been easier. His attempts to communicate seemed to be getting more urgent, but what on earth did he have to say that was so damned important? After half an hour of that painful nonsense, I'd end it with some fatuously cheerful line like, "Well, Dad, time for more coffee?" and he'd give up, turn away from me, and stare at the silent TV.

Then I would shut myself into the back bedroom (where it was always over ninety degrees by then), sit at my mother's sewing table, and stare at my neatly stacked four hundred pages. Had I been enough of a writer to have writer's block? Maybe it was impossible for me to do any serious work at home in Raysburg; maybe I could only write in distant cities, dreaming of home. And it was not lost upon me that if it hadn't been for my father with his wild and wooly tales of the first John Henry Dupre riding with Morgan the raider, I never would have started writing that goddamned novel in the first place. Maybe it was *my father* who was too close. I found that wreck in the next room inordinately depressing.

Dear old Dad, of course, had been the original fat drunken buffoon. He'd never allowed himself to get as fat as I was, but he'd always been a big, jolly, red-faced, sweating, plump man who'd never minded tucking into a good plate of roast beef or fried chicken—and drunk certainly, every damned day, and a buffoon often. We'd loathed each other when he'd first come home from the war, but we'd learned to make allowances for each other, and there'd been times over the years when we'd genuinely liked each other—or, at any rate, I had liked him and hoped that he'd liked me. He'd never hit me, drunk or sober, but the rages that sometimes drove him until I was sure he was getting *close* to hitting me had always happened when he'd been sober as a stone, and I found myself—with a twinge of embarrassment—remembering one of those times. He'd come home early from work, and he'd caught me wearing that tartan skirt I'd insisted was a kilt. He'd chased me all over the house, yelling his head off, until my mother had rescued me with her usual, "He'll outgrow it."

If he had been drunk, he might have found it funny. I'd never minded him drunk. When he'd been drunk, he'd always liked me.

In fact, I was often the only one who could deal with him then, and more than once I'd been the one who'd talked my silly-ass father into going to bed. My mother always said that I was better at it than she was.

The night my father heard that *his* father had died, he came home monumentally loaded at damned near five in the morning. I knew something was up because I heard an enormous crash as loud as if somebody had knocked over a dresser. I jumped out of bed and ran straight downstairs, found my father flat on his back on the kitchen floor. He'd managed to fall over without, apparently, spilling a drop of the whiskey in the glass that was resting squarely in the center of his chest. He was staring bleakly at the ceiling, smoking a cigarette, and using the cat's dish for an ashtray. "Do you want to go to bed, Dad?" I said.

"Yeah." But he didn't move a muscle.

I sat down on the floor. "Shouldn't walk around. Bare feet," he said. "Catch cold." He sounded as though he was trying to talk with a mouthful of mashed potatoes.

He was right: it *was* cold on the kitchen floor. I remembered crossing my legs and tucking my feet under them. I could sit that way for a long time and liked to do it because I knew it was something grownups couldn't do. My father was trying to look at me. Even though I was only a few feet away, it took him a while to locate my face. The whites of his eyes were red; the lids were swollen. He sipped some of the whiskey. "Hey, Johnny," he said, "how the hell old are you now?"

"Ten."

"Yeah, that's right. Forty-two you were born. That's right . . . Do you remember your grandpa Dupre?"

"Sure."

"Did you like him?"

"Sure."

"Well, he's dead."

"I know. Mom told me."

"Yeah. Shit. My dad. Good man. Wish I was half the man he was. Shit. What a way to go. Shit. Well, let's drink to him."

He handed me the glass. I knew that if my mother was there to see it, she'd drop as dead as my grandfather. I took a tiny sip, fought to get it down. It felt like swallowing a lit match. I felt it burn down my throat, burn through my stomach, and stop at the bottom in a little pool of fire. But I didn't cough. I was proud of myself, gave him the glass back.

My father downed the rest of the whiskey, and that seemed to focus him. He looked me straight in the eyes. "You can be any damn thing you please in this sorry life," he said. "Just one thing I ask of you. Always remember who you are."

I tried to make sense out of that. "Who am I?"

His eyes shot fire at me. "You're John Henry Dupre the Fourth, that's who the hell you are."

AT TWENTY-THREE I still didn't have any better idea who John Henry Dupre the Fourth was than I'd had at ten, and whatever thoughts my father had on the subject, I certainly wasn't going to be hearing them. One evening after dinner, I decided to ask my mother about the Dupres. "I don't know much about them," she said. "You should talk to your grandmother."

"But she's not a Dupre. What happened to those old people who used to come visit? There was O. E. and Aunt Myrtle and Uncle Will . . ."

"Oh, honey, they're all dead and gone now. O. E. died just last year. He was never right in the head, poor old soul. Gassed in the First War . . ."

"Was he? Why didn't I know that?"

"You weren't much interested in family when you were little."

That was true; I hadn't been. "But my grandfather," I said, "the professional gambler . . .?"

She laughed. "Is that what your father told you? His dad wasn't a *professional* gambler. He was just a gambler period. He worked his whole life at Elwig's Tobacco. He was a cigar maker. He'd get paid on a Friday, and if your grandmother didn't get to him first, he'd lose every cent of it in a poker game. That's why she left him."

I was feeling a familiar frustration; had my father ever told me the simple unvarnished truth about anything? "OK," I said, "but how did Grandpa Dupre end up in *Lexington, Kentucky*?" The home of John Hunt Morgan.

"His health was failing him, and he moved there to be close to his daughter . . . You remember your Aunt Matty, don't you?"

"Yeah," I said, although I wasn't sure I did. "Why was *she* in Lexington?"

"I don't have any idea. You really should talk to your grandmother."

I would have liked to talk to my grandmother, but she wasn't living on the Island any longer. She'd come undone while I'd been in L.A. It had started out with her phoning in the same order to the grocery store four or five or even ten times a day. Then somebody had called the fire department about the thick black smoke pouring out of her apartment, and the firemen had found her calmly watching television while the stew she'd left on the stove burned to cinders. Eventually her phone and electricity had been cut off because she'd forgotten to pay the bills. All the time I'd been growing up, when I hadn't given a damn whether I talked to her or not, she'd been two blocks away from us; now that I did want to talk to her, she was twenty miles down the river in Carreysburg, living with my Aunt Evie and Uncle George. "Does she still make any sense?" I said.

"Oh, she makes perfect sense so long as you've got her back in the old days. Just don't ask her what she's had for breakfast."

"Maybe I will go see her, but . . . Mom? You know all those stories Dad used to tell about the first John Henry Dupre? How he was from New Orleans, killed somebody in a fight . . . rode with Morgan in the Civil War? Do you suppose any of that's true?"

"I don't have any idea if it's true or not. He told me the same wild yarn . . . I wouldn't put too much stock in it. Your father never could tell a story without improving on it."

Yes, he had been a great spinner of yarns, a great improver of stories, but it was odd, I thought, what he chose to turn into legend and what he didn't. I'd heard a million times about the first John Henry, but I couldn't remember my father ever saying a word about what he'd done in *his* war. "Did he ever talk about being in the navy?" I asked my mother. "Did he see any action?"

"Action? You mean fighting? I don't think so . . . They took his age into account, trained him as a radio operator. That's what he did all through the war. To this day, he can still understand Morse code. Didn't he ever tell you that? He was on one of those boats that moved cargo around, don't think he ever got within a hundred miles of a Jap. He said he'd never been so bored in his life. He and some of the other sailors made a little still and ran off their own liquor." She shook her head with that sadly complex look I'd come to know over the years—both proud of my father and his arcane abilities and utterly disgusted with him. Then, probably worried that she'd sounded disloyal, she added, "Oh, but your father was always so much fun. That's why I married him."

"So how'd he get in the navy? Was he drafted?"

"Oh, good heavens, no. A few days after Pearl Harbor, he and Bernie Andrews got themselves three sheets to the wind and enlisted."

I laughed. She smiled back at me. "It wasn't all that funny at the time. Bernie failed the medical, but your dad didn't . . . and I didn't appreciate it at all. He was thirty-four years old, for crying out loud. And I was seven months pregnant with you. He didn't *need* to do that."

That's just great, I thought. He was an even bigger asshole than I was.

LYNDON JOHNSON was having a televised news conference that week, and I wanted to watch it, God knows why. I even got out of bed early for it—that is, before noon—and made sure that my father and I were planted in front of the tube in plenty of time, our coffee cups filled and our cigarettes lit, but then the damn thing started late. "What do you think of all this stuff, Dad?" I said.

He made that harsh coughing sound he used for a laugh. "Ssslowa crap," he said. That had come through clearly enough, and I laughed along with him. Then, after an interminable wait, the President of the United States appeared on the screen, staring straight at us, beginning, as he always did: "Mah fellow Americans . . ." All I had to do was hear that cretinous voice—I RIDE FROM TEXAS ON A BIG WHITE HORSE—to be sickened, once again, with a noxious hatred for the lying son of a bitch. "Not long ago," he told us, "I received a letter from a woman in the Midwest. She wrote, 'Dear Mr. President, in my humble way I am writing to you about the crisis in Vietnam. My husband served in World War II. Our country was at war. But now, this time, it's just something that I don't understand. Why?'"

He then proceeded to explain it all to us. It was, just as my father had predicted, a load of crap. I put up with it as long as I could, and then I started yelling back at the TV set. "This really is war," LBJ said.

"Yeah," I yelled, "so why wasn't it declared in Congress?"

"It is spurred by Communist China."

"No, it's not. Jesus. Why don't you try reading a history book?"

"Its goal is to conquer the South, to defeat American power, and to extend the Asiatic dominion of Communism."

"Bullshit. They were fighting the French and now they're fighting us. All they want is to run their own goddamn country." My father must have thought I was funny. I kept hearing that coughing noise out of him. I was glad I could make him laugh.

"Because we learned from Hitler at Munich that success only feeds the appetite of aggression."

"Jesus Christ, Lyndon," I yelled, "Vietnam is not Nazi Germany."

I sat there and fumed. Now LBJ was telling us that he was raising the number of men in Vietnam from seventy-five thousand to a hundred and twenty-five thousand. "This will make it necessary to increase our active fighting forces by raising the monthly draft call," he said, "from seventeen thousand . . . to thirty-five thousand." I felt the deadly impact of that just as though he'd whipped out a hidden six-gun and blasted me with it.

I survived to the end of the speech. I even sat through the question period with the press. But I wasn't doing any more yelling at the TV. The number was staggering—*thirty-five thousand per month*. What were the chances of some month's thirty-five thousand not having me in it? "Do you want me to leave the TV on?" I asked my father.

"Nuh . . . John?"

Oh, God, I thought, not today. Please, not today. "I'll talk to you later, Dad. I got to go."

He gave me a reproachful look and an explosive gesture that looked like "fuck off." I ran downstairs and began walking (waddling) up Front Street toward town. *Thirty-five thousand, thirty-five thousand.* WALK DOWN TO THE LIBRARY, PICK UP YOUR MOTHER'S CAR (AND SOME MONEY), AND DRIVE TO MORGANTOWN. No, that's stupid. I wouldn't get there before the Registrar's office closed. OK, THEN CALL THEM FIRST THING IN THE MORNING. Yeah, I'll do that. Of course that means I'm definitely sending my poor mother back to Household Finance, which is the last thing in the world she needs at the moment. How did I get myself into this fucking mess? Oh, this is intolerable, intolerable.

I'd taken off just like the guy I used to be—the guy who would walk anywhere, walk off his sorrows, walk all night long, walk for *pleasure*, for Christ's sake, but, panting and dizzy, I was gradually slowing to a shuffle, and I hadn't even made it to the bridge yet. I hauled out my handkerchief and mopped my face. Every sweat gland in my body was in excellent working order, and I was stopped just where I didn't want to be, in front of our old house; as I always did when I passed by it, I looked up to see again the little balcony where I used to stand for hours, imagining that the shitty feelings I was having were making me more poetic. And then, of course, I had to walk by Cindy's house. In memory, we're sitting on the floor and she's wearing what she wore to school, a blouse and a pleated jumper, and I'm wearing the same thing— although that's certainly not what *I'd* worn to school. Or, if we're acting out some more exotic fantasy, she's in an old dress of her mom's and I'm in a old dress of hers, and she's playing a grown-up version of herself—that is, the ruler of this magical kingdom—

and I'm playing Princess Somebody-or-other or, as I often did, simply "little sister."

Ah, but these obsessively detailed, embarrassing, and even somewhat queasy memories would lead me, as I knew full well by now, nowhere but straight back into my old labyrinth—come on, son, LET YOUR MIND ALONE—and I was halfway across the Suspension Bridge by then. Once again, I'd been slammed to a stop. The sun was a blacksmith's hammer, and I was the anvil. Below me, just as sad and fat as I was, the old brown Ohio reflected back a hideous dazzle; my sunglasses were at home on my dresser, and the light screwed me squinty-eyed. Where was I going? Did it matter? ASK NOT, ETC. I watched a barge push a load of coal up the river. I was halfway to town so I might as well keep on going. I plodded on across the bridge and down Market Street to the five-and-dime where I appeased the hollow inside me with a hot turkey sandwich, an extra side of stuffing, and a strawberry milkshake.

Gorged into torpor, I stepped out into the disgusting sunlight, flinched back instantly to the tiny patch of shade in front of Kresge's, lit a cigarette, and watched the parade of afternoon shoppers, mostly female—schoolgirls happily out of school, teenagers, moms and kids—and, by God, it really was just as weird as I'd thought: the middle of a West Virginia heat wave and half the girls on the street were strutting around in go-go boots—not wearing them with short skirts like the girls in L.A., but with shorts, just the way in any other summer they'd be wearing sneakers. For the grade-school crowd, they appeared to be as essential as coonskin caps had been in the mid-fifties. Moms had put them on five-year-olds—and on themselves. Zoë had told me that when she'd first worn those little white boots, people had turned to stare at her on the street, but now Lyndon's majorettes were everywhere.

Thinking of Zoë, I dragged myself on up to Middleton's on Chaplin Street, stepped gratefully into the raw shadows of the place, into the familiar stench of darkroom chemicals. A stand-up fan that looked like something from the forties wheezed at the end of the counter. The owner himself was in today: "Hi, son, hot enough for you? What can I do you for?" I didn't know why people called him "Doc," but they did, and it fit him—a dapper old gent in a bow tie, probably in his eighties, bald-pated as porcelain but sporting a trim white goatee. He was a famous photographer (or, at any rate, as famous as you could get in Raysburg), had photographed a president once (I didn't remember which one, Harding maybe), and he always did the graduation pictures for the boys at the Academy. Mine was still hanging in our living room; if you bent close, you could see that the great man himself had signed it in pencil: "S. Middleton, 1960."

"Hi, Doc," I said, "D & C for Dupre."

"Dupre? Didn't you graduate from the Academy a few years back? Yeah? I thought I knew you. Put on a little weight since then, haven't you?"

"A pound or two," I said, annoyed.

"Happens to the best of us," he said, although he looked as though he hadn't gained an ounce in sixty years. He passed me an envelope. I took out my contact sheets, spread them on the light table, and bent to study them through the loop. Zoë, in black and white, leapt up into my right eye. Damn, she looked fine. But the late afternoon sun had been burning through that hole in the hedge like a flamethrower, and half the image was lost in a hazy white flare. Why hadn't I seen that? "Shit," I said under my breath.

I did a quick pass over the contact sheets, and it was obvious that I had not distinguished myself. That flare I should have noticed ruined many of the outdoor shots. I'd been afraid to move in close to define the image; my framing was as safe and haphazard as if it had been done by somebody's mom with a Brownie. I should have crouched down to emphasize Zoë's fabulous long legs (especially in her Courrèges copy dress), but my fat stomach must have discouraged me from attempting anything that arduous. In the fading light of the dining room, I'd been fully aware that my depth of field had been reduced to nothing, but even so, I'd been out of focus half the time, or had focused on the wrong thing, got the crochet stocking on one of Zoë's legs as sharp as an etching but allowed her eyes to blur out to pointless pools of fuzz. There were half a dozen shots that were better than anything she had in her book so far, but that wasn't saying much. Zoë always looked great. It seemed impossible to take a bad picture of her. But she could have used a far better photographer than the idiot who'd shot those seven rolls of film.

"Excuse me, son," Doc Middleton said, "could you use some advice?"

"Sure," I said.

I stepped back and let him look through the loop. "Pretty girl," he said.

"Yeah," I said, "she wants to be a model."

He looked again. "You know, she might be able to do it . . . just not here in this town. She ought to go to New York, or at least Pittsburgh."

He didn't seem to have much to do, and I didn't either, so I let him explain to me the humiliating details of every dumb mistake I'd made. Then he showed me one of his studios at the back of the store. It was exactly like Mr. Feinstein's (although a hell of a lot cleaner)—a roll of seamless on the wall, two lights on stands with umbrellas, and a minuscule change room. "Tell you what," he said, "this is the slowest time of the year for me. Picks up in

September, but it'll be dead as a morgue right on through August, so I'd be happy to rent it to you. How about five bucks an hour? If you wanted it a whole afternoon, I could give you a better rate than that. You'd never have to worry about your exposure. You'd be shooting at f 22, so you'd never have to worry about your depth of field. All you'd have to worry about is the girl."

I'D BEEN dropping in at the Markapolous household for five years. I was, as I'd been told often enough, *a member of the family* and therefore not someone who was expected to knock, but now, confused by an arcane dread, I paused on the porch, uncertain of myself, wishing that I *could* knock—so someone would come to the door and be glad to see me, would greet me warmly and invite me in. I heard voices, laughter, the TV, the humming of fans, and a faint strain of Zoë's rock 'n roll drifting up from the basement. Usually I would have called out, "Hey, anybody home?" but I didn't do that. I opened the screen door slowly so the spring wouldn't squeak, slipped on through, eased the door shut behind me, and slunk into the house as quietly as a horse thief. Not sure why I was playing that childish game, I tip-toed on down the hall-way to the living room and stopped just inside the archway.

Revington and Cassandra were sitting close together on the couch. One of his hands was resting innocently, almost absent-mindedly, on one of hers. The good doctor was holding court from his usual position on his recliner; all he had to do was raise his eyes from Revington's face and he'd see me, but, for the moment, nobody knew I was there. Pretty good, I thought, for a fat man.

Revington was in full flight: "Astute . . . very astute. I was impressed. The bombing will keep the Republican hawks off his ass. Going to the UN will keep his own left flank off his ass. And then there was the direct appeal to the American people . . .

couched in plain language that anyone could understand . . ."

"Here's where we differ," the good doctor said, interrupting. "What you admire is exactly what I don't admire . . . I know damned well he's a good politician, but the last thing in the world we need right now is a good politician. We need a *statesman* . . . Hey, there, John, grab yourself a beer and get in here."

I was pleased to see Revington jump as if a spider had bitten him. "Ace," he said, turning toward me. He'd been struck, for once in his garrulous life, utterly speechless.

I saw Cassandra get the whole picture in a flash. She grinned at me, dropped her eyes significantly to Revington's hand on hers, then looked up again, looked me straight in the eyes and winked. I didn't have a clue what she'd meant by that, but I grinned idiotically back. "Thanks," I said to the doctor. "I brought Zoë her contact sheets," waving the envelope in the air as though it gave me diplomatic immunity, "but I'll take the beer though," and in LBJ's peckerwood accent: "Y'all know what I think anyway."

"That's never stopped you before," Revington said. It was, I thought, a fairly lame line for him. He jerked his head in the direction of an empty chair, sending me the message: "Just get your ass in here and sit down, for Christ's sake."

"There's only one thing that troubles my mind," I said slowly, deliberately. "It's my old Waterbury, and she won't keep time." Leaving them with that one to ponder, I drifted into the kitchen. Damn, I was going to have to figure out how to get Cassy alone for a minute so I could find out what was going on.

Zoë didn't hear me coming either; she had her radio turned up full-blast and was talking on the phone. I waved her contact sheets at her. She squealed—a sound like YOW!—and said, "I'll call you back later. John's here with my pictures," and to me, "Show me, show me, show me. Are they any good?"

She might, I suddenly realized, have trouble looking at them; like an idiot, I'd forgotten to buy her a loop. "It's OK," she said, "I'll get Dad's magnifying glass," ran upstairs and was back with it before I'd even decided where to sit.

She turned her radio down to a bearable level, cleared a space in front of her sewing machine—pushing away scraps of plaid fabric—flicked on a lamp, and motioned for me to join her in the pool of yellow light. Reluctantly, I pulled up a chair. "Wow," she said, "some of these are kind of . . . What is that?"

"Flare," I said. "I was trying to use the sun as a back light. Sorry."

"Oh, but here's a good one. Hey, it's really good." She offered me the glass. I brought the image up into strong magnification. It was one I'd passed over because her face looked so blandly and unremarkably pretty, but, taking a moment to look again, I could see why she liked it. THE LOOK came through clearly—exactly what she'd wanted when she'd said "prissy"—scrubbed, polished, every hair in place, every detail perfect from gloves to purse, and it dawned on me (somewhat late in the game, I thought, for someone who'd been hooked on girls' magazines since he was fourteen) that fashion photography isn't about *the girl*; it's about *the clothes*.

"Can I get eight-by-tens?" she said.

"Oh, sure. Just mark the ones you want."

We spent an hour going over her contact sheets. Half a dozen times I was tempted to tell her about Doc Middleton's studio, but I didn't. I was beginning to suspect that I shouldn't be taking any more pictures of Zoë. She was wearing, as she usually didn't, a fairly strong perfume—if I'd been writing ad copy for it, I might have called it "sassy"—and I didn't think of myself as someone who was susceptible to scent, but that perfume was really getting to me. But wait a minute—on second thought, who was I kidding? Of course I was susceptible to scent, and her perfume was very much like Natalie's; in fact, it might even have been the same damned thing—and by now, a lot more was troubling my mind than my old Waterbury. She was such a goddamn lovely girl, and I liked her, could even say that I admired her, and here we were, crammed together, cheek to jowl, peering through a magnifying glass, and I was acutely aware that she was the very same girl I'd kissed under the mistletoe a couple years before, the very same girl who'd recently starred in one of the most unsettling of my frequently unsettling dreams. But Zoë was not quite sixteen, and I was twenty-three, forty pounds overweight, and very definitely not in the right place at the right time. "I'm going to get another beer," I said. "You want anything?"

"Oh, if you're going upstairs . . . a Coke."

I went looking for Cassandra, found her on the front porch glider with Revington. Ordinarily I would have been stepping into the middle of a conversation, or perhaps one of his political monologues, but when they'd heard me coming, they'd stopped talking—instantly, BANG, curtain going down. He had one of his arms wrapped around her, and she was leaning back against his shoulder. "Having fun with little sister?" she said.

"We play very nicely together," I said and got a laugh from her.

Behind Cassandra's line of sight, Revington gave me a heavily weighted look and the thumbs-up sign. I nodded back to him—bobbing my head like an end-man in a minstrel—and wandered away, into the house, considered joining the good doctor and his wife in the living room, thought better of it, got a beer and a Coke, and headed back to the basement. What kind of tom-foolery was playing here tonight? Should I set it to music? That thumbs-up had meant exactly what? Had Revington already won his bottle of

Scotch or did he think he was right *on the edge* of winning it? "I got the new *Seventeen*," Zoë said. "You want to look at it?"

I'd thought she was offering it to me so I could look at it by myself, safely isolated in my own chair, but no, I gathered that I was supposed to sit next to her on the couch so we could look at it *together*. That was something I needed like a bullet in the brain. The cover of *Seventeen* proclaimed that it was THE BIGGEST FASHION ISSUE EVER!

"We were right," she said smugly, "all the skirts are short. Every single one. A lot of them are up to here." With a pink frosted fingernail she drew a line on her leg a good four inches above her kneecap. "Look, even the girls in the ads," and began flipping through the pages.

"Hey, do you see this?" she said. "That's THE LOOK I want . . . I don't mean for a picture, I mean for real." The girl in the magazine was wearing a costume that said most emphatically, I AM A TEENAGER—blazer, sweater, ribbed tights, little-girl flats with straps, and a short pleated dotted skirt that ended exactly where Zoë had just drawn the line on her leg. The girl, like Zoë, wore her hair in a pageboy; like Zoë, she had bangs, but hers were so long they were almost in her eyes. She was wearing more makeup than Zoë usually did and was staring directly at us with an expression that was disturbingly self-possessed, faintly menacing, and eerily engaging. I understood perfectly; if I were a teenage girl, that's exactly how I would want to look too. "You could do that," I said. "You're practically there already."

"Yeah. I could. I can see it in my mind. It's just getting everything right. I love it when everything's right and it all comes together . . . Oh, I sound so superficial, don't I? That's what Dad's always saying to me, 'Don't be so superficial, Zoë.' Well, we can't all be brains . . . He's kind of spoiled, you know, with Cassy. She really is smart. He thinks everybody should be like that, but most ordinary kids aren't like that . . . Hey, do you think I'd look better as a blonde? I don't mean Marilyn Monroe blond, I mean a dark honey blonde. I'm so close, I'd just have to go one shade lighter. Dad would kill me. Do you think I'm superficial?"

"No," I said, laughing.

"Yes, you do," she said, giggling. "I can tell. You're thinking, oh, my God, what a little pin-brain."

"No, I'm not, Zoë. I'm really not."

"Do you think I'm silly . . . trying to be a model?"

I thought that she had a one-in-a-thousand chance, but I didn't think she was being silly. She had a better chance than most girls. "No," I said, "if there's something you really want, then go after it."

"That's what I think too."

"Why do you want to be a model?" I really wanted to hear what she would say.

She looked up from the magazine and into my eyes. "I don't know . . . I can't . . . I guess it's just something you *feel*. Haven't you ever wanted something just because you feel it?"

"Oh, yeah," I said with conviction.

She flipped through a few more pages. "Oh, John, look at this skirt! My God, isn't it just *fab*ulous? It just kills me." The skirt was black patent vinyl. "God, if I wore that in Raysburg, people would drop dead on the street. But I'm going to make it, I swear I am . . . if I can find the fabric. You see how simple it is. It wouldn't be hard to make . . . Oh!" She was off the couch in a leap, turning up the radio. "It's my favorite song." It was the Dave Clark Five belting out "Over and Over."

"Come on," she said, "dance with me."

"I'm a fifties guy. I never learned the new dances."

I watched her dancing. She looked heartbreakingly young. I had told her the truth; the way the kids were dancing now seemed impossibly alien to me, made me feel as though I was not merely a few years older but from an entirely different generation. When the song was over, she turned the radio down and fell back onto the couch. "Don't worry so much about your weight," she said. "When you decide to lose it, you will. Are you really going back to WVU?"

I was so astonished I couldn't speak for a moment. Anyone who thought that Zoë was a pin-brain was making a serious mistake. "I don't know," I said.

"Dad says you're in limbo. He says you haven't found yourself yet."

I laughed reflexively. "Well, it's not because I haven't been looking."

"Oh, I know. But you're smart. You'll figure things out." She picked up the *Seventeen* again. "Look, do you see how all the lips are really defined now? Cassy's so out of it. Those chalk-white lips look really dumb."

"She's got her own style. She's the cat who walks by herself."

"Yeah, that's what she thinks, but after a while you can look really dumb. That beatnik look is out now. If she let me, I could make her look like a dream. Don't worry about *her* either. I don't know what she's doing with him, but I know she's not serious. Does it bother you?"

Impolitic or not, I could not possibly deflect a direct question like that. "Yeah, it bothers me."

"I thought it did. It'd bother me too . . . I guess you just have to pretend you don't care. Sometimes she's just . . . I don't know. Just out of it. Do you like the Scotch plaids? Some of them are really *really* short. Look at that one. Wow."

"What's the perfume you're wearing?" I heard myself stupidly saying.

"Oh? Do you like it? I really like it. It's called F Sharp. You're the first person who's noticed."

"I really like it," I said.

She looked at me, and I looked at her, and for one excruciating moment we just sat there with our eyes locked. Oh, God help me, when I'd been barking like a dog and chasing her up the street, what *exactly* had I been yelling? It would have been nice if those particular words had been blurred away into the Lethe of minty bourbon, but I, unfortunately, remembered every preposterous one of them. Zoë could have been deeply offended. She wasn't acting like someone who had been deeply offended. She'd thought I was funny. ("Oh, but your father was always so much fun.") What else might she have thought? What was she thinking *right now*?

Suddenly, with no preamble whatsoever, she jumped up and began demonstrating poses for me. "See, the catalogue girls are just standing around. That's all you have to do. But the editorial girls really have to show the clothes . . . bring them to life. Miss Fairfax says you can tell the amateurs by their hands." She made her hands into awkward fists to illustrate her point. "It has to look simple and easy even if it's not." She skipped across the room and back, her arms floating gracefully outward, sending me a dazzling smile.

"I should have a camera," I said.

"Oh, God," she said, "sometimes I want to grow up so bad I can taste it."

AND WITH that—I thought somewhat later, sitting with a six-pack on the river bank—Zoë had most emphatically put an abrupt end to my somewhat limited social life. The next night I wandered around my parents' apartment after dinner feeling increasingly restless and bitter. I did not want to watch a rerun of Johnny Yuma with my father or try to have yet another desultory and unfocused conversation with my mother while she sat in bed and read a Readers' Digest Condensed Novel. I did not want to look up my pals from high school. I did not want to get drunk alone at the Yacht Club. I withdrew into the back bedroom and, as usual, saw it stacked neatly there, waiting just as patiently for me as it had been doing for weeks—the four hundred pages of my unfinished and very definitely *not* condensed novel. Ever since I'd seen the rotten peckerwood on television, I'd been hearing at my back the sound of Lyndon Johnson hurrying near (thirty-five thousand, thirty-five thousand), and what did I think? That I had all the time in the world? Then I was struck by one of those deceptive flashes of insight that can convince you, at least momentarily, that you're as brilliant as Einstein: it had been crazy to consider working in the hideous afternoon heat, but there was nothing stopping me from working in the cool of the evening.

OK, I told myself, it's now or never. I got out my old battered briefcase left over from my days at WVU, packed my manuscript and four freshly sharpened pencils into it, and walked down Front Street to the Yacht Club. I knocked back a shot of bar whiskey, bought a quart of Stroh's, and settled down at my distant table overlooking the river. There was a good hour or more of daylight left. I was sick with apprehension. After putting it off so long, I couldn't believe I was finally going to read the damned thing. I admired my title page: THE REST IS SILENCE. I'd always loved that title page. It looked so real. But I couldn't simply sit there getting drunk and staring at my title page. I had to read all those goddamned words I'd written.

I felt a growing sense of dismay. God, this shit was terrible. I remembered how hard it had been to get the book going, and it certainly showed in the writing. My style kept changing. The opening was like an awkward attempt to sound like Zane Grey, but then I'd abruptly shifted into a peculiar tough-guy voice. I'd thought of it as a Confederate Hemingway, but now I saw it as more like a hillbilly Raymond Chandler. Finally, after fifty or so pages, I'd settled down to imitating what I'd taken to be the grandly mellifluous prose of the mid-nineteenth century. But style had been the least of my problems. I'd started half a dozen scenes and then abandoned them with the note: FILL IN LATER. After many scenes I'd written an even more maddening note: DO WE REALLY NEED THIS? (In most cases, the answer to that was a resounding NO.) The facts of Henri Leblanc's life kept changing; I didn't seem to be able to remember, from one scene to the next, even how old I'd decided he was. I'd interrupted the story periodically to give the reader long lectures on the history of broadside ballads in the hills of Western Virginia. (I'd written these in a tone of pompous authority, but I'd made most of it up.) Worst of all, my mountain folk were absurd cardboard cutouts with not a spark of real life to them. Ah, the pigs, the incest, the flintlock rifles, the moonshine stills, the mindless violence, the ancient feuds, the utterly ridiculous way the people talked: all of it was as phony as a thirty-cent coin. The denizens of Dogpatch had more reality to them than any of the grotesques I'd created.

Was *this*, I asked myself, what I'd spent a year and a half of my life doing? Was *this* what was going to justify my existence, excuse me for being a horny and perpetually frustrated peripatetic fuck-up, an unemployed leech on my overburdened mother, a draft-eligible university dropout, a Buddhist Confederate and a fat drunken buffoon? OK, I thought, now wait a minute. Would I lose anything if I threw away the first hundred pages? No, not a goddamn thing. The book really started at Chapter Four.

I would never forget the weekend when I'd begun writing Chapter Four. For months my shabby little room had been crammed with library books: Civil War histories, Civil War dictionaries, social histories, memoirs and letters, even histories of fashion. I'd been writing slowly, painfully, a tortured paragraph at a time, but I'd been spending much of my free time reading. Then, suddenly, my writing achieved critical mass. The strange style I'd adopted began to come easily to me, almost naturally, and the writing poured out in a fiery torrent. I stopped reading because I was too busy writing. I was no longer floating on the surface of my story; I *was* the story. I wasn't lonely anymore. I didn't need anybody. I had my crappy job and my crappy room, and that was enough because I had a whole other world—a vivid, compelling, absolutely real world with real people in it. I could hardly wait to get off work so I could plunge back into my beloved other world; I longed for the weekends so I could spend two whole days there. And I'd continued to write in that compulsive frenzy right up to the moment when Mr. Feinstein had told me with genuine regret that he wasn't making enough money to keep on paying my salary. To hell with all this preliminary crap, I thought, and flipped through the pages until I found what really mattered.

CHAPTER FOUR: RUMORS OF WAR

For weeks, Leblanc had been suffering in this northern spring; at home the days would already be thick and full of the promise of summer, swelling with the rank fertility engendered by the great Mississippi, the sun above the levee leaping daily into a renewed sky like the most brilliant of banners, unfurled, promising victory if one were only to follow, but here in Kentucky nothing was familiar. Here in this alien land where Leblanc had found himself, as always, an exile, the afternoon sun was thin as a watery lemon punch, throwing a false warmth that vanished by twilight. Here clouds unrolled in high sinister patterns above the strange bluegrass and cast a bitter viridian light as Leblanc busied himself with his daily affairs. He had endured the cold driving rain that had awakened in his breast that ancient melancholy which appeared to be his eternal lot. His sinews were tensed for a perilous adventure that was woefully slow in arriving, and his heart was filled with foreboding. "Ah, the ladies," proclaimed Captain MacGillivray with a wink. "We, sir, have been too long deprived of the society of ladies. Let us ride."

And ride they did, Leblanc on his trusty mare, MacGillivray on his spirited stallion, at a full rattling gallop down unknown roads. Leblanc felt his spirits, too long constrained, lift and soar. The pale afternoon light of rainy Kentucky, the old familiar feeling of the leathers in his hands, the dark thunder of the hooves beneath him, his own youthful flesh moving in sympathy with the powerful beast between his thighs, the very blood coursing in his veins: all of this tumbled together to lead him to a moment of realization that life was again, and indeed would be, again and again, a thing of glory. Ahead of him, MacGillivray slowed his steed to a walk. As Leblanc drew abreast, MacGillivray extended one languid arm, offering a silver flask. Leblanc took it and tasted the finest of Kentucky sour mash whiskey. He laughed.

"Tenting tonight, boys, tenting tonight," sang MacGillivray and then laughed also. "Ah, sir, do you see it there . . ."

As they rounded a bend in the road at the crest of a hill, distant signs of human habitation emerged below them in the gathering twilight: what appeared to be a small town. MacGillivray withdrew his watch from his coat and consulted it. "A splendid ride we've had of it," he said dryly. He stretched out his long arms, settled back in the saddle with the easy air of a man who has spent most of his life on horseback, glanced at Leblanc with a sardonic smile. "I know your heart, sir," said he; "The destination is entirely a matter of indifference to you . . . just so long as you are riding."

Leblanc returned the smile. "As to that matter, you, sir, do indeed know my heart."

"But all roads must have some destination, and this is ours."

As they walked their horses down that final hill in the blue evening, Leblanc saw that what was emerging from the gloaming was not, after all, a town, but a manor commanding the curve of a quiet river. The pattern of the grounds was perfectly circular; paths led outward from the hub of the great house with its Doric columns to many smaller buildings, some of which, Leblanc thought, must be the servants' quarters. Swallows darted low to the grass before them, and, high above their heads, a nighthawk cried out in its melancholy raucous voice. The encroaching night had colored the mysterious scene with evanescent shades of grey and dun; the slow curve of the river shone like nacre. Leblanc could hear the faint strains of music, see yellow flames of candles flickering in the windows. There appeared to be a hundred carriages drawn up on the grounds.

"And what is this destination?" asked Leblanc.

"You, sir, surely have heard of Charles Tuberville?"

"Indeed. Who has not?" Charles Tuberville was one of the wealthiest men in the state; the Tubervilles were entwined with the Morgans and the Hunts and all of the most ancient fortunes of old Kentucky.

"Well, yonder lies his modest manse," said MacGillivray, "and tonight is the grand ball." Then, seeing consternation written plainly on his companion's face, he added:
"The ladies, my dear fellow. You said that you had been

far too long denied the society of the ladies."

"But sir . . . I have also been denied an invitation."

"An invitation? Who says that I have received an invitation? They cannot forbid us access. The Tubervilles have always known the MacGillivrays."

As Leblanc sat in his saddle, sorrowing and uncertain, MacGillivray shrugged, then shouted out: "Fear nothing, Leblanc!" With a harsh laugh, he was gone, kicking his stallion into full gallop. "Damn his eyes," Leblanc thought, but he was left, as always, with no recourse but to follow.

IT WASN'T quite as good as I'd remembered it, but I had caught *something*—I could feel it: an intensely powerful charge of emotion—but would anyone else feel it? What if the emotions I'd experienced while I'd been writing hadn't made it onto the page? And if they hadn't, how would I ever know? And then, of course, there were all the details I hadn't bothered to check. Did Kentucky really look like that? Who knows? I'd never set foot in the state. There must surely have been swallows in nineteenth-century Kentucky, but nighthawks? I'd put them in because I'd always loved those damn birds with their distinctive rasping voices; they flew around in the twilight skies of Raysburg, and they'd been in my mind as long as I could remember—like the river—but was there a river in Lexington or anywhere near it? There might be, but I didn't know; I hadn't even bothered to look on a map.

And the horses had given me the fits. I'd never been on a horse in my life . . . well, unless a pony counted. When I'd been six or seven, my parents had taken me to a county fair where they'd had a pony ride for children. The ponies were so old they could barely place one hoof in front of the other; the kids were plunked on them and led around by a friendly old farmer, and my father decided it was something I should like because that's the sort of thing boys were supposed to like. He wanted to take my picture on the pony, but I was terrified of the pony. My mother was off with some women friends, so it was just me and the old man locked in a battle of wills. Looking back, I could feel a certain sympathy for him. Here was his son: a tiny, underweight, horribly shy little boy who spoke in a girlish whisper and used impossibly big words (*nebulous* is the one I remember stopping him in his tracks)—his son who played with girls, preferred reading in his room to running around in the sunshine, and who did things like cutting roses from patterned fabric and sewing them neatly onto black velvet. Goddamn it, that rotten little sissy was going to ride the pony! He picked me up under the arms and set me down in the saddle. Weeping, I sat on the pony throughout one interminable circuit of the field. My father took a picture of me weeping on the pony and then set me back down on the blessedly firm earth. I started to sneeze, and I sneezed nonstop for ten minutes. My eyes swelled shut and my hands and neck broke out in hives. As I would find out years later when I would be subjected to a battery of tests, I am violently allergic to horses.

Did my absolute ignorance of horses show in my writing? "A full rattling gallop" had been the best I could do, but if you were writing about the Civil War, you couldn't really avoid horses. Maybe I could read some books on riding or talk to people who rode—or maybe it wasn't important. *The emotions* were what counted, and when Eleanor Tuberville entered the book, the emotions soared straight up into the stratosphere—well, at any rate, *my* emotions had soared that high. Now I skipped the long description of the ball at the Tubervilles' and turned directly to what I was sure must be one of the most powerful and significant scenes I'd yet written—that nearly mystical moment when Leblanc first meets Eleanor.

Leblanc cast his eyes about, located a span of wall that was occupied by no one, withdrew into it, removing himself from the gay assembly. He wished to be excused, for the nonce, from the demands of social intercourse. How many more times, he wondered, was he destined to stand at the back of some grand crowded room, having already, in spite of any of his past resolves, imbibed far too deeply of strong spirits, his thoughts rearing and stamping like a hot blooded thoroughbred eternally restrained in the starting gate? The musicians struck up the next tune, and the laughing dancers flowed into the graceful pattern of a Virginia reel. "Mon Dieu," Leblanc thought, "those men play well!" The two venerable Negroes, one sawing splendidly on a fiddle, the other beating a banjo with ecstatic abandon, were the best musicians of their kind he had ever heard. Men who played like that deserved to be free, he thought -- and Leblanc looked up and saw that a young lady on the far side of the room was watching him. It was not the first time that he had noticed her, seen her somber grey eyes searching him out. He would have expected any young lady of breeding to look away when his eyes met hers, but she did not look away; neither did she smile. In contrast to the animated figures whirling before her, she was standing stock still as though she had composed herself for the making of a tintype.

Leblanc allowed his eyes to continue to rove about the room as though they had paused on hers purely by accident; then, as he turned his head, he found Captain MacGillivray regarding him with a glittering smile of wicked amusement. "You are not dancing, sir."

"I lack the grace," Leblanc said, although he had cut a splendid figure in many a ballroom in New Orleans. "That lady yonder," Leblanc said. "Standing alone off to one side . . . the one who is, at this very moment, regarding us . . . Who is that young lady?"

MacGillivray took Leblanc by the arm and led him along the margins of the room in the direction of the lady in question; laughing, he said sotto voce, "Scarcely a lady yet, hardly more than a child, wearing, I daresay, hoops for the first time in her life . . . Our ladies marry young in Kentucky, but for this one, my dear sir, you will have to wait as long as Jacob for Rachel," and then, pitching his voice to the rhetorical heights of a stump orator, he said: "Mistress Tuberville, would you allow me to present to you my friend, the redoubtable Captain Henry Leblanc, late of New Orleans. He is, I assure you, a splendid fellow, and he has . . . if you will forgive my saying so . . . expressed a fervent desire for the pleasure of your acquaintance."

Leblanc did not know whether to be most distressed by MacGillivray's florid speech, by the discovery that this slender feminine creature was the youngest daughter of Charles Tuberville, or by having heard himself so unexpectedly promoted to a mythical captaincy. "I am most pleased to make your acquaintance, Captain Leblanc," she said, her low voice as somber as her eyes.

Discomfited, Leblanc relied upon deeply ingrained habits of courtesy, brought his heels sharply together, bowed, took the hand of this exquisite young girl -- for, indeed, that is what she was -- and raised it partway to his lips. "Mademoiselle Tuberville," he said. "I am enchanted."

"Ah," she said. "Parlez-vous Francais?"

"Oui," he said, surprised, "bien sur."

"How do you find the society in our fair state?" she asked him, speaking in French.

He answered her in French: "I like the society in Kentucky very much . . . now."

He had hoped to elicit a smile from her, but his hopes were dashed. Regarding him with her splendid eyes, she reverted to her native tongue: "Would you care, sir, to stroll in the gardens? Here it is still and close, and I feel myself oppressed."

She took the arm he offered her, and, as they made their way toward the great doors that had been thrown open to the cool evening air, he availed himself of the opportunity to examine the young beauty. Her lustrous chestnut hair had been curled into tight ringlets and bound back with a blue ribbon; her gown was also blue, the color of the sea at the coming of nightfall. She might be, he thought as he regarded the clarity of her small ovular face, little more than a child, but she was already no stranger to whalebone: he could have spanned her easily. Her skin was pale, nearly as white as velum, but scattered over with a faint spray of freckles, betraying, perhaps, an active girl who had eschewed the parasol. She possessed, he believed, the most beautiful eyes he had ever seen, enormous and shining; they, however, revealed nothing of her inner thoughts, but her cheeks were flushed prettily as though under the pressure of some strong emotion, and he saw, in the firm set of her little jaw, what he took to be apprehension. He continued to wait upon her smile, and he continued to wait in vain.

To the tune of her rustling petticoats, she led him down the paths of the formal gardens where the light was fading, and he fancied that soon the heavens above them would assume the fairy color of her dress. She carried a fan but did not open it; perhaps she was not yet schooled in such coquetry. "Have you come here to join in preparations for the great contumely?" she asked him.

He wondered if she were making a jest at his expense, but her eyes were grave. "Yes," he said. "I have come to ride with Morgan."

She regarded him with a steady gaze; still she did not smile. "I fear," she said, "a great effusion of blood."

OBVIOUSLY THE scene still needed some work. As compelling as I'd found it, the Kentucky I'd created didn't seem to be subject to the same laws of nature that constrained other less magical locations. It had been twilight when Leblanc and MacGillivray arrived at the Tuberville's, and it was still twilight an hour or so later when Leblanc goes for a stroll with Eleanor. What? The sun never sets in Kentucky? And formal gardens? Where the fuck were we, Versailles? And then there was Eleanor's tiny waist. Leblanc could span her—*easily*? I made a circle of my fingers. Jesus, that was small. Nobody could possibly have a waist that small. And hoopskirts had given me as much trouble as horses. I'd studied the illustrations in the fashion books, so I knew exactly what a set of hoops looked like and how it worked, but I didn't know what it was like to *wear* a hoopskirt. How on earth did you sit down? When you did sit down, what happened to your skirt? How close could you stand to a gentleman, or, for that matter, to another lady in a hoopskirt? How could you dance? What happened to your hoopskirt if you were walking outdoors in a strong breeze? Did anyone ever get a chance to see your shoes?

But it wasn't merely a matter of this detail or that detail, horses or hoopskirts; I was afraid that the whole thing was a load of crap. I sat there by the river reading until the sun set in nonmagical West Virginia. Then I moved inside to the light of the bar and read the rest of it. The whole thing was a load of crap.

I was so disappointed that it took at least an hour, and a lot more beer, before I could even begin to think about what had gone wrong. I considered that famous, iconic, touchstone story about Hemingway; he's at an outdoor café in Paris (at least that's how I remembered it), and he's trying to write *one true sentence*. Well, at least I could console myself with the thought that I *had* written one true sentence: "I fear a great effusion of blood."

What in God's name had I been doing? When I'd made my Confederate stump speech to Revington and the good doctor, I'd predicted that Texas Lyndon would divide the country as it hadn't been divided since 1861, and I'd been right. I'd begun writing my novel out of admiration for the cantankerous, rebellious, independent spirit of the Confederates—their willingness to stand up to the Yankee war machine—but, much more to the point of *my* life and times, it was the Vietnamese who were now, at this very moment, standing up to the Yankee war machine. The great effusion of blood had already begun, and my country was sinking into waste and damnation, and what had I been doing? I had just spent a year and a half in a Romantic haze glorifying men on horseback. Oh, shit: I RIDE FROM WEST VIRGINIA ON A BIG WHITE HORSE.

H O W M U C H had Vietnam colored my strange writing? How much had Vietnam influenced the way I thought about the Civil War? Much more, I suspected, than I had known at the time. I had never felt as strongly about any public issue as I did about Vietnam. There were no shades of grey for me, no complexities. Whether viewed through the lens of simple morality or that of realpolitik, the war was stupid and wrong; it ran counter to every American ideal I'd been taught in grade school; the longer it went on, the more deeply I felt about it until it came to represent for me everything that was wrong with America—a tragedy, an obscenity, a national disgrace from which we might never recover. A number of different forces had brought me to that conviction. I'd read histories of Vietnam, knew about the traditional Vietnamese mistrust of China, knew about French colonialism. I'd read accounts of American foreign policy, knew about our Cold War fondness for backing repressive right-wing dictatorships. I'd been gratified to see my high-school hero, Allen Ginsberg, protesting against the war. I'd followed the public debate; as much as I'd detested him, I'd voted for Lyndon Johnson, the peace candidate. It had seemed right to me, even inevitable, that Martin Luther King should come out against the war. But the emotional core of my feelings, that rock-solid certainty, centered on an image I had seen on television for only a few seconds, would see later in a famous still photograph.

Cohen and I were in the small room that we'd shared in his uncle's hotel in the spring of 1963, watching the eleven o'clock news to see again what we had already seen on the six o'clock news—the image of a Buddhist monk burning himself up in Saigon, a man sitting in a perfect lotus position, unmoving, as flames consumed him. I felt again the same visceral horror I'd felt the last time I'd seen it. That image changed me in a fundamental way, as the photographs from the Nazi death camps had changed me when I'd been a boy. The reporters who covered the story did not dignify that burning monk with a name, and it would not be until years later that I would learn that his name was Thich Quang Duc, that he did not move a muscle or utter a sound as he burned to death, that the Buddhist monks and nuns had been distributing leaflets calling for the government to show charity and compassion to all religions. American reporters at the time covered the event as though it were merely a protest against the anti-Buddhist policies of the Diem government—a regime that I knew was vile, repressive, corrupt, and supported by the United States. But Cohen and I saw in that image of the burning monk something far more significant.

On some level (as Cohen would have said), we were both Buddhists. Looking back now, I can see how half-baked and silly we were—as Cassandra once called us, "a pair of Buddhist Boy Scouts"—but we were trying at least to practice Right Action. Vietnam was a largely Buddhist country. That burning monk was not some impossibly distant alien figure to us; he was our brother. When I saw that burning monk, I knew that the United States of America had no business in Vietnam in any capacity whatsoever.

Although we had to be up early the next day for the morning shift, Cohen and I walked on the beach behind the hotel until long after midnight. The sea curled in with that swoosh and roar I could admire but never quite love because the Ohio River didn't do that; the moon was reflected in the sea. Miami Beach was too beautiful, too peaceful, too perfect, too far from Vietnam. Cohen and I walked up and down on the smooth sand for an hour, neither of us saying anything. Then, suddenly, I knew what to say; I was amazed that I hadn't thought of it before: "All is burning. And what is all that is burning? The eye is burning, visible forms are burning . . ."

I couldn't remember much more of the Sutra than that, but Cohen, smiling, completed the opening: "Visual consciousness is burning, visual impression is burning, also whatever sensation, pleasant or painful, or neither painful nor pleasant, arises on account of the visual impression, that too is burning. Burning with what? Burning with the fire of craving, with the fire of hate, with the fire of delusion . . . burning with birth, aging, and death, with sorrows, with lamentations, with pains, with griefs, with despairs."

We walked farther without speaking. We were both of us, I'm sure, still thinking of the Sutra; as many of them do, it continues on as formally as a theorem in mathematics, telling us that sound, smell, taste, touch, and even consciousness itself is burning. A monk who understands that everything is burning loses attachment to these manifestations—and we were both still thinking of the burning monk in Saigon.

"Being dispassionate, he becomes detached," Cohen said in his oddly singing voice. "Through detachment, he is liberated. When liberated, he knows that he is liberated. Birth is exhausted, the holy life has been lived, what was needed to be done was done, and there is nothing left in the world."

IV.

I DROVE south. I could have picked a better time than the middle of the afternoon; the damnable sun was doing its worst in a blazing scum-white sky. I cruised through Center Raysburg—my father's old stomping ground—passed those legendary few blocks where, in the old days, every door in every back alley had hidden a whorehouse or a shady all-night club. Holding at a steady thirty-five to catch all the lights green, I drifted through South Raysburg where Lyle and my other Polish pals had grown up, and on down to Millwood, past the blast furnace and streets as bleak as anyone's worst imaginings of East Berlin; then the city gradually trickled away into empty lots and warehouses, weeds and scrub burnt brown by the sun. I hit open country, began to see the endless series of mills and chemical plants pouring out their steady stream of pollution. Without rain to break it, wind to move it, that layer of pale filth had piled up and persisted, squeezed us down into these wretched claustrophobic dog days of August.

I was following the old river road. The Ohio, sludge-brown with chemical wastes, rolled along on my right. I passed through Scottsbog and on into county jurisdiction, pushed my mother's Dodge up to ninety and held it there. This road belonged to the sheriff, and everyone knew that he had better things to do than worry about speeders. I was, I knew perfectly well, on a fool's errand—not driving to Morgantown to register for the fall semester (as I'd been telling myself to do every morning for days) but on my way to the dumb little river town of Carreysburg to try to figure out just who the hell John Henry Dupre the Fourth was.

Carreysburg didn't have much of a downtown. I went into the drugstore, found a lunch counter, had a cheeseburger and a milkshake, asked directions to the cemetery. It was off a road that wound its way up the hill above town. Driving there, I passed the little red brick building with a sign telling me that it was the local of the United Steel Workers of America; I found the cemetery just where I'd been told it would be—stretching out over a hilltop overlooking the river. The town must not have been able to afford to water the place; the grass had been seared as yellow as a tobacco stain, and the sun was truly ghastly; I hadn't walked ten yards before my entire shirt was soaked. I felt stifled and oppressed, and it didn't help that the entire universe pulsed with the ancient, monotonous, querulous hum of locusts. I plodded over to the nearest grave marker, an ornately carved, well-weathered marble obelisk about three feet tall with a circle carved into the face of it; inside the circle, a disembodied hand pointed directly upward, presumably in the direction in which the spirit had departed. The grave beneath was that of MARTHA ANN *wife of* THOS. MORGAN. She'd been born in 1786 and died in 1848. Christ, I thought, that was a long time ago. And this was supposed to be the *new* cemetery. I'd been told that the oldest graves were down by the river where many of them had been washed away. And then I thought, *Morgan?* Oh, shit. I already knew what I was going to find.

The cemetery was packed with Morgans. Here in this dumb little West Virginia river town, these were certainly not the relatives of the wealthy John Hunt Morgan of Lexington, Kentucky. I began looking for my own relatives. Other than Dupre, the only name I knew in my father's family was Owen (my grandmother Dupre had been an Owen), and I found plenty of them; there were almost as many Owens as Morgans. Then—and I'd almost walked right by his low stone—I found my great-grandfather: JOHN H. DUPRE. It was, of course, my own name, and I stared at it, feeling an obscure dismay. He'd been born in 1838 and died in 1906. Next to him was his wife: PERNILIA E. DUPRE, 1846–1932. I kept on walking, following the slope of the land downward, and found recent Dupres, some of them the old folks I remembered from my childhood. There was my batty uncle, or great uncle, or whatever he'd been to me, identified in death as he had been in life, only by his initials: O. E. DUPRE. He'd died when I'd been in L.A. Just inside the wrought iron fence, I saw my own name again, this time written out in full: JOHN HENRY DUPRE. I hadn't expected to see him there. It was my grandfather, returned home from Lexington, Kentucky: 1872–1952. Surprised, I felt my eyes stinging with tears, and I knew that I'd been writing the wrong story.

I kept wandering around reading names on stones. I didn't know what else I was looking for; I'd already found enough. Then, on a tall column, I read the names of the four children of EDWARD OWEN: MARTHA, JOHNATHAN, EDWARD, and MARY. The youngest had been two when she'd died, the oldest seven. He'd lost all four children in the third year of the Civil War. To what? Diphtheria, measles, the flu? How sad, I thought, and then I was leaning on the column weeping like an idiot. Could I really be crying for these dead kids who might not even have been related to me? I was angry at everybody in that goddamned cemetery for being dead. I wanted to pop them out of their graves so I could ask them questions. Who were you? Where did you come from? What did you do here? What was it like to be alive?

AUNT EVIE and Uncle George had a nice old house right on the river. The paint was flaking off and the front porch was sagging, but it was so much like so many of the houses where I'd grown up that it felt homey and familiar. "Your grandma may not know who you are," Aunt Evie told me, "but whoever she thinks you are, she'll be glad to see you."

I stepped out into the little sun porch overlooking the river and saw that my aunt and uncle had done their best to recreate my grandmother's favorite room just the way it had been in her apartment on Raysburg Island. Grandma sat in the same old rocking chair in front of the same old table where the Bible and the last few issues of *The Readers' Digest* were lying, along with a box of stationery, some postage stamps, and the same little basket with her emery boards, bottle of clear nail polish, pincushion, scissors, thimbles, and several spools of thread. Her African violets were lined up along the window. Her porcelain Persian cat regarded her from an end table. She must have been to the hairdresser recently; her white hair had been neatly permed. My first impression was that she wasn't really *that* old—her skin seemed remarkably unlined—but when she rose to greet me, I changed my mind. It was a struggle for her to get up. Her entire body was shaking with a small but constant tremor. "Oh, Johnny, it's so good to see you." She gave me a hug. In my arms, she felt tiny and moist. She settled slowly back into her rocker. I sat in a straight-backed chair directly in front of her. "How is everybody?" she was saying, "How's Dotty and the boy?"

Oh, I thought, she thinks I'm my father. "I *am* the boy," I said and then realized how odd that must have sounded. "I'm not John your son. I'm John your grandson."

She gave me a sharp accusatory stare and then turned decisively away from me. She rocked and looked out the window. "They ain't a shippin' on the river the way they used to," she said after a while.

Then she turned back and looked at me again. She reached out and patted my tummy. "You sure ain't missed a meal, have you, honey? Are you still going down to the university?"

Relieved, I laughed. "I used to, Grandma, but I don't anymore."

"That's right. I knowed that. Your father had that stroke, didn't he? A few years back? Ain't that so? How's he doing?"

"He's not too bad, but he still can't talk very well. He doesn't get around very well."

"Is that so? It's a shame. I should get over to see him. But he ain't the only one who don't get around much. You know, Johnny, I don't hardly ever get out of this apartment. Nobody talks to me. Getting old's not much fun; I can't recommend it to you. You're too young to carry all that weight. All that fat, it wraps around your heart and squeezes it . . . The trouble with your father was he never could say no to a glass of whiskey . . . I should go see him. Well, I reckon I could get Mary to take me over there. She wouldn't mind doing that. She's always been good to me."

Mary Roth had been my grandmother's neighbor all the time I'd been growing up; I remembered her as a large cheerful red-faced woman who used to give me ginger cookies with raisins in them. She'd been dead now for five years or more. It was sad what had happened to my grandmother; she'd grown up in Carreysburg, so, in a sense, she'd come home, but she thought she was still on Raysburg Island. "Grandma," I said, "can I ask you some questions about the Dupres?"

"You should go talk to your uncle Ogden. He's the one that knows all about the Dupres."

Oh, I thought, so that was O. E.'s name. "I can't. He died last year."

"Did he? That's a shame, that's a shame. You see how it is, nobody tells me nothing. People seem to think I don't have good sense."

"Well, we all know you have good sense, Grandma . . . I just wanted to ask you . . . Do you remember the first John Henry Dupre? Your husband's father?"

"Well, of course I remember him. There's nothing wrong with my memory. There's people around here think I'm getting senile, but they've got another think coming. I told Evie that I wasn't going to go live in one of them homes. I'd die first. 'You can't live alone anymore, Mother,' she says. Well, hell, I've lived alone now for . . . how many years has it been? What year is *this*?"

"Nineteen sixty-five. Grandma . . .?"

"I won't put up with it. I told her that too. Right to her face." She rocked furiously and stared out the window.

I felt as though I were trying to dig a hole in a swamp. Would it do any good to remind her that she was living with Aunt Evie and Uncle George? No, probably not. "Grandma," I said. "The first John Dupre . . . ? Your father-in-law? What kind of man was he?"

She didn't even stop to think about it. "Oh, a nice man. Always something nice to say. Well liked. The salt of the earth. A nicer man than his son, if you want to know the truth." She grinned and winked at me.

"What did he do for a living?"

"He went on the river same as all the boys."

"Do you remember his wife? Pernelia?"

She laughed. "Nobody called her that. They called her Aunt Penny. I called her 'Mother.' She told me she'd be honored if I called her 'Mother,' so I always called her that. They was good to me."

"When Grandpa died," I said, "he was in Lexington, Kentucky."

"That's right, he was."

"How did he get there?"

"He went there to be near to Martha."

"That's your daughter?"

124

"Yes. They was always close."

"How did *she* get there?"

"Well, you see, she married a Kentucky boy, and he was in the First War, so they had to give them preference. You know, for the jobs. He was from Ashland, and there weren't no jobs there, so he went to Lexington and got hired on at the post office. Worked his whole life for the post office."

Well, I thought, that takes care of that. There really was no connection whatsoever between my family and John Hunt Morgan. But I wanted to be absolutely sure. "Do you know if the first John Dupre was in the Civil War?" I asked her.

"Oh, Lord no . . . It was old Billy Morgan was in the Civil War."

"Was he a Confederate?"

"No, Union. Weren't no Confederates around there. Everybody was Union. Old Billy Morgan and some of the boys in them days rode around and made sure the river stayed safe."

"They were in the state militia?"

"I don't know what they was in. You'd have to ask Ogden. He could tell you that."

Here we go again, I thought. Well, all I could do was push on and see how far I could get. "Do you remember the story that Dad used to tell . . . about how the first John Dupre came up from New Orleans and rode with Morgan the raider?"

I was expecting to hear her deny having heard any such thing, but she laughed and said, "Oh, yes, I heard him tell that one many a time. He loved telling that one. I always told him he should write some of them stories down . . ."

"But there wasn't any truth to it?"

"Oh, good Lord no. You didn't think it was a true story, did you? Well, he fooled you good then. He was always doing that.

He loved to do that. Yes sir, he was a pistol, all right. Started making things up when he was . . . oh, I can remember him coming in the kitchen, not tall enough to get his nose over the edge of the sink, and him telling me about how the spiders was having a war with the bees . . . don't know what all. Always had the gift of the gab. And then after he got to reading . . . He always was a good reader. Got good marks in school. Should have gone on to college, but that was the Depression, and nobody was going nowhere . . . But there was this one book he read when he was little, all about sword fights and French people, and he went around telling everybody he was a count. French royalty. Told people he was related to the queen of France. You know, the one they cut off her head? Had half the boys on the Island believing it too."

"So the first John Dupre wasn't in the war?"

"Good Lord, no. I already told you that, honey. I don't think he was even in the country then."

"During the Civil War?"

"Yes, during the Civil War. That's what we're talking about, ain't it? Some people around here treat me like I don't have good sense . . . The Dupres come down after the war was over. Looking for work. Some of them stayed up in Pittsburgh and worked in the steel mills there, but John and his brother went on the river. There was a landing down in Carreysburg back in them days. The packet would come in, toot its horn, and whatever you was doing, you'd drop everything and just come a runnin' . . ."

"Wait a minute, Grandma. So where were they during the war? France?"

She looked at me as though I'd just been transformed into the village idiot right before her eyes. "France? Good Lord, honey. The Dupres was from Canada."

V.

THE WEATHER did not break, several hundred anti-war pro-
testers were arrested in Washington, race riots broke out in Watts,
and I did not drive to Morgantown. I sat night after night at the
Yacht Club, staring at the river. Heat lightning blistered the sky,
and when it did, I'd wait—sometimes it felt like forever—until I
heard, far off in the hills, a low mumble of thunder, but we never
got a drop of rain. All of my identities had melted away in that
vile summer's vile heat; I'd given up looking for any reason to do
anything. One morning I found the letter lying innocently on the
floor below the mail slot. I knew what it was before I opened it.
I'd been expecting it, yet I felt a shock wave that surged through
my entire body and prickled my scalp. Greetings! ASK NOT
WHAT YOUR COUNTRY CAN DO FOR YOU.

I called Revington. "Christ, William, I've been drafted."

There was a long pause. Then he said, "Well, I hope you'll
serve with honor."

I hung up on him.

He called me back immediately. "That was the wrong thing
to say, huh?"

"Yeah, that was the wrong thing to say." I realized that somewhere along the way I'd lost the ability to tell the difference
between Revington serious and Revington kidding.

"Well, John, it was bound to happen eventually. You knew
that. Now you can stop worrying about it. It must be a relief. I
wish things were that simple for me."

"Oh, shit."

"I'm still not certain that I'll be entering law school in the
fall."

"Oh, shit!"

"I mean it, John. We might be *there* together."

"Cut the crap, William, you're home free. If they get on your ass in law school, you can always marry Alicia."

He said nothing. "Christ, man," I yelled at him, "this is fucking serious. This isn't just another scene from *Casablanca*."

"I know that, Dupre."

"I'm thinking of going to Canada." I hadn't been thinking about it, at least not seriously, but I thought I'd try it out on him.

There was another long pause. Then he said, "That's the most ridiculous thing I've ever heard."

"Why is it ridiculous?"

"What is there in Canada?"

"I don't know. I haven't got there yet."

"I'll tell you what there is in Canada. Nothing. What the hell are you thinking about? You're going to be some kind of expatriate like Hemingway? Well, Canada's not Paris. And you'd be a goddamn exile. You'd never be able to come back. Do you understand that? Christ, you're not serious, are you?"

"I don't know."

"You'd go nuts in Canada, for fuck's sake. You wouldn't know anybody. You wouldn't know where the hell you were. It *is* a foreign country up there, you know? You'd never see any of your friends again."

"Yeah," I said.

"Or your parents."

"Yeah," I said.

"It's fucking cold up there," he said. "They're having their winter now."

I had to laugh in spite of myself. "It might be fun . . . a new beginning."

"Oh, a new beginning, my royal Canadian ass! You're not

128

going anywhere. You're going to stay here and do your duty like a man." I RIDE FROM TEXAS TO ENFORCE THE LAW.

"What is that crap?" I yelled at him, my voice flying away hysterically. "Fuck you, asshole. Do you ever believe *anything* you say? You sound like a parody of a parody."

"You don't like that one, huh?" he said.

"No, not much."

"OK, how about this one? You had most of the goddamn summer to do something about it, but you didn't do a goddamn thing. You pissed around and pissed around and now it's caught up with you. That's life, man. I'm sorry for you, but what the hell did you expect? You're going in the army because you haven't got any choice. It's that simple, OK? Yeah, it's a fucking stupid piss-ass war. Yeah, we never should have got involved over there. But we did. And we're stuck with it. Jesus, John, I'm sorry . . . I'm terribly sorry . . . but what the fuck do you expect me to say? Just do the best you can. That's all you can do. Try to impress them with how smart you are, and maybe they'll put you behind a desk."

He was right. Everything he said was right.

I SHUT myself into that terrible back bedroom, chain-smoked, paced up and down, drank cup after cup of coffee, and stared at the draft notice lying on my mother's sewing table next to my failed Civil War novel. No matter how many times I read that goddamned letter, it always said the same thing.

In the afternoon I called Cassandra, but I got Zoë. "John! We've missed you. Yeah, really. Cassy keeps saying, 'What's with old Dupre, where's he got himself to?' and I . . . Oh! I'm *sixteen*, can you believe it? They threw a surprise party for me and I didn't even . . . but they had balloons and everything . . ."

I felt old and weary and hopelessly distant from Zoë's

sparkling voice: ". . . just like you're supposed to, a pink cake with sixteen pink candles, wow, you should have . . . *Surprised?* Was I ever! And Cassy found me the vinyl, you know for the patent skirt I showed you, she had to *go to Bellaire for it*, it's going to be . . . and some neat fall clothes, I was *touched*, you know, and, *oh*, Jeff gave me a charm, now I have eight, real gold, I said, 'You didn't have to,' and my dad . . . *the Dave Clark Five album*, it's just fab, and my mom, some nice fall sweaters and you know how mom, underwear and stuff like that, oh, John, I'm so excited, *now I can get my driver's license!*"

Right, I thought, her sixteenth birthday, a big deal, and I probably should have got her something, but I'd forgotten all about it. I couldn't take her today. I had to get her off the phone. "Happy belated," I said. "Is your sister there?"

My tone must have stopped her. She took a breath. Her voice went flat and formal: "Well, no, not at the moment. She went off somewhere with William. I don't think she's going to be gone too long. Do you want her to call you?"

"No. It's not important."

I walked on up to Belle Isle and sat on the river bank in the lethal sun. If this wasn't *in extremis*, I didn't know what was, and I needed to talk to somebody. It seemed strange—maybe I could even call it *tragic*—that when it came down to the crunch, there were so few people who really mattered. I could call my mother at the library, but what was the point of that? She'd be home in a few hours. And I hadn't talked to Cohen in over a year; I didn't even know where he was. Eventually, I dragged myself back to the apartment, walked in and saw my father sitting where he always sat, doing nothing, smoking the occasional cigarette.

I threw myself on the bed in the back bedroom. The heat in there was appalling, but I lay on my back and stared at the ceiling.

Once you'd been drafted, could you register in school and then request a reclassification? Somehow I didn't think it worked that way—not when they needed thirty-five thousand men a month. Now what? Revington was right; I'd run out of options. Why the hell wasn't Cassandra home? I couldn't think straight. I really did need to talk to somebody. I'd never felt more alone in my life.

Eventually it occurred to me that I should tell my father—just to get it out of the way so I could move on to the next thing, whatever that might turn out to be. I got up, walked into the living room, and sat down next to him. Ordinarily I would have boomed out some stupid line in my heartiest voice—"Well, Dad, how are you doing?"—but I couldn't do it. We sat there side by side and looked at the silent TV.

I'd come in quietly, and I wondered if he'd even noticed. "John?" he said.

"Yeah?"

He produced another of his spitty splatterings of words. I couldn't make out anything. Oh, this is intolerable, intolerable. I got up, moved my chair around until I was facing him, and sat down again. He wiped his mouth with the back of his good hand. "John?"

"Yeah?"

He tried it again. I stared straight into his face. He was looking back at me, his dead eye glassy and strange, his live eye watery and blinking. He was trying his damndest—trying so hard that I could see the good side of his face vibrating with the effort of it. Then, for the first time since I'd been home that summer, it struck me how terrible it must be for him. What if his mind was the same as it had always been? The immaculately groomed tomcat with the gift of the gab, the spinner of fabulous yarns, the zany cackling joker, the good-time Charlie, the glad-handing con-man who'd always had a good word for everyone—trapped inside the prison of his body, unable to communicate? I couldn't imagine anything worse. "I'm sorry, Dad," I said, "I'm just not getting it."

He sighed and fell silent. Sitting there simply looking at him began to feel increasingly embarrassing—difficult, unnerving, and strange. Every instinct told me to get up, turn away from him, and walk away. I don't know what kept me sitting in that chair—perhaps the thought of how similar we were, something I'd always hated to admit. It was so quiet I could hear the fans going in every room. I felt lines of sweat trickling down my sides. It was cruel what the stroke had done to his face, how one side seemed perfectly normal while the other was like an unconvincing mask. I could see him looking back at me. I couldn't imagine what he must be thinking. His eyes were a lot like mine, nearly the same shade of brown, but he was wider at the jaw than I was. There was something hard to define—a quality, a sympathy—in the expression of his good eye that I recognized as mine. Most of my life, he'd felt like a stranger who'd appeared out of nowhere, but he really was my father. And *now*, God help me, could I get up and leave? I wanted to. I'd been there long enough. I'd done my duty, hadn't I? But no, it seemed that I had to continue to sit there and look at him. His good eye was watering heavily now. Could he be crying? Oh, God, I didn't want him to be crying. That would be too cruel and embarrassing. I should say something. But what the hell could I say? I said the first feeble thing that popped into my mind: "Dad? What's the matter?"

He smiled with the good side of his face. He took a deep breath and tried it again, but all that came out was yet another unintelligible splatter. He took several breaths, and then, spacing out his words carefully, trying so goddamn hard to be clear, he said something that I could make out: "I hate this."

"Yeah, I bet you do," I said. "I think it's the shits. I'd hate it too."

"John?"

"Yeah?"

"You oh kay?"

"Yeah," I said, "I'm OK, Dad. I'm going to be OK."

His good eye was really watering now. He wiped the moisture away with the back of his hand. "Mmmm, mmmm, mmmm," he said. I leaned closer. "I'm sor ry," he said.

For the length of a heartbeat I was suspended in a bubble outside time. Then I said, "It's OK, Dad, you did the best you could."

He took his good hand and pressed it against his heart. "Stu pid," he said. Then he pressed his hand against my heart. "Don be stu pid."

THE NEXT day, while I was trying to pack, the storm that had been prowling around the valley finally hit us. I'd been hearing the wind all morning; it had been whistling in the fireplace in the living room; it had been making the roof groan. Violently driven sheets of rain blew up from the river, pounded the walls and rattled the windows in their frames. I dug out an old raincoat from the back of the closet, found my cowboy hat from my Morgantown days, and ran down to the riverbank. Lightning scrawled across smudges of blackened sky over the hills above town; in less than a second, the thunder shouted back. The storm was passing directly over me. I smelled the weirdly twisted burn of ozone; lightning was striking close (and I would find out later that a tree on the South End had been struck), but I didn't care. The rain was hammering down my hat; the thunder seemed to be roaring up from the earth directly beneath my feet. I loved the sense of danger, the loose electricity, the roiling chaos—with me right at the center of it. Then the storm blew past, leaving behind a steady talkative rain. I paced up and down and smoked and felt the temperature drop. The valley had been transformed from dog days into slate-grey autumn. The ghastly heat was gone. This is all right, I thought. This is more like it.

I hadn't felt so exhilarated in months, maybe even years. I hurried back to the apartment and headed straight for the basement. I was determined to do what my mother had been asking me to do all summer: *go through my things*. I found twenty or thirty dusty cartons stacked up in the storage locker; when I began to open them, I saw that my mother had imposed no order whatsoever on that mess when she'd packed it up for me. There were clothes stuffed in with books stuffed in with papers stuffed in with every damned thing I'd left lying around in my room in the old house: used guitar strings, electrical cords and plugs, shoe polish, cuff links, hair brushes, several pipes and some dried-up tobacco, stones from the river bank, records, candles, incense, a small brass Buddha, notebooks, childhood art work, old report cards, photographs, chess sets, my old track shoes, the stamps I'd collected in the third grade, *everything*. It felt as though I had to put my whole life in order—which, of course, is exactly what I had to do. Revington had been right: I'd been pissing away my time all summer—I'd been pissing it away for years—but I'd been caught. The long tall Texan was not just one jump behind me; he was here, and every second now had to count for something. I was ruthless. I threw away most of that crap.

I saved anything I felt might help to sustain me—a precious collection of fragments from my previously discarded selves: the Manila envelope with all of the terrible but painfully sincere poems I'd written between the ages of twelve and fourteen, and, in another envelope, the high-school poems I'd always thought were "mature" but I saw now as just as terrible and far less sincere; the nutty weight-height charts I'd tried to match at fourteen when I'd starved myself below a hundred pounds because that's what a girl with "a light frame" was supposed to weigh; and, still glued to the cardboard I'd used to support it, the Salutatorian's speech I'd read at my graduation. I threw away most of my medals from the Academy, but I saved the ones for riflery. Just as it always did, that strange picture of me dressed as Alice in Wonderland on Halloween when I'd been seven filled me with a queasy dread, but I knew I had to keep it—along with my Morgantown notebooks and the pictures I'd taped to my walls in my last dire days at WVU. I remembered how I'd rearranged those pictures with me as Alice at the center, how that pattern had, mysteriously, represented my whole life. Now I had to rearrange things again, find a new pattern. These artifacts, fragments, had no value in themselves; they were the records left behind by the powerful lines of force that had surged through my life—and that was how I was thinking about my Civil War novel now, not as an uncompleted work of fiction but as another record of a difficult time I'd survived.

"Consider," Rilke had instructed me so long ago, "the Hero sustains himself; even his downfall was an excuse for his continuing existence, his final birth," and I did consider it. The hard edges and bright shapes of the world were springing up into high relief again, and I could feel the great lines of the world in motion again. I knew that I was at a gathering point, so maybe there was a way out of this shit. Maybe the Hero hidden inside the fat drunken buffoon could sustain himself yet again and be reborn.

The only person I wanted to talk to was Cassandra, and where was she? Never at home when I called, so I stopped calling. The girl who had never played games with me was playing games. Well, I could play games too.

I didn't know why, but Zoë was someone else who was on my mind. I knew I'd hurt her feelings on the phone, but that was trivial, wasn't it? Of course I'd been abrupt, dismissive. I'd just got my draft notice, for Christ's sake. It had never crossed my mind that I could tell Zoë about it. But why was I worrying about her feelings when my entire life was changing? I felt a line of force pulling us together—not in the way I'd thought that Cassandra and I were linked, at the level of soul, and certainly not in a sexual way—but linking us nonetheless. My book had not been a success; I wished Zoë well with hers, and I found myself remembering that ridiculous line from *Lawrence of Arabia* Revington had been muttering all summer. Wouldn't it be good if, before I left Raysburg, I could find *something honorable*?

I'd done everything I had to do. I was almost out of time—but not entirely. When I called the next day, I expected Zoë to answer the phone, and she did. "Cassy's not here," she said. I heard her take a breath. "I'm really sorry you got drafted."

Oh, I thought, Revington must have told everybody. I almost said, stupidly, "It's OK," but caught myself. How ridiculous could you get? "It's happening to a lot of guys."

"Yeah, it's horrible. I hate this war, just hate it. It's all so stupid and wrong. It's *immoral*. I really am sorry."

"Thanks. I appreciate that. I'm trying not to think about it right now . . . Look, Zo, I'm not calling for Cassy, I'm calling for you. I'm sorry I missed your birthday, but I've got a present for you . . . if you want it. I can get us a studio over at Middleton's for a couple hours. Do you want to make some pictures?"

She didn't answer for so long that I was afraid I'd crossed an invisible line into forbidden territory. Then she said, "You're kidding."

"I'm not kidding."

"What do you mean, a studio? A real one? With lights?"

136

"Yeah, lights and all. It's not that big, but . . ."

"Oh, my God, you're kidding."

"No, I'm not kidding. I've got some time, and if you're not doing anything . . ."

"Oh, my God, I'd love to. Tell me you're not kidding."

"Hey, just one or two outfits, OK?"

When I pulled up in front of the Markapolous household, Zoë was waiting for me on the front porch, her hair up in rollers and wearing a pop-art raincoat so trendy she must have bought it in Pittsburgh. She pulled the hood over her head and ran through the rain to the car. I stepped out and grabbed her suitcase and tackle box; she gestured toward the porch, and I scurried up to get her father's camera case. She was talking before I could even get the car in gear: "I can't believe this, I really can't, I thought you were kidding, I wasn't doing anything, thank God I did my nails last night. My hair! Good grief, it's never going to dry, I got it as dry as I could but, tried to think what, we already did back-to-school, and the summer's over so I don't want to do any flowy, you know, some-enchanted-evening, and go-go boots are out, they're still showing them but they're kind of like *for children* now, and then I just looked out the window, all this rain, I thought it's just like fall, and I, hey, I finished the patent skirt, it was a real drag to sew but it fits like a dream, I mean it's fab, I mean just supercool, and I thought fall, fall sweaters, Argyle, and then I thought, oh, right, that's it, LET'S DO THE COVER OF *SEVENTEEN!*"

Doc Middleton greeted me as though I were an old and val-ued customer. "Sure, it's all yours. You've got till five-thirty, how's that?" We agreed on a figure, and I paid him. He sold me six rolls of Agfa, ushered us into the studio, and left us alone there. The modeling lights created a small, self-contained, brilliantly lit world. Zoë let her suitcase and makeup box fall to the floor and stood, frozen, staring at the huge silver umbrellas, at the pale grey seamless. Surrounded by darkness, that patch of lit emptiness was going to be her stage. We heard the rain hammering the building. I tried to imagine what she was feeling. "You must have seen all this stuff before," I said. "It's pretty standard."

"Yeah, when we did our head shots. But I was with a whole bunch of other . . . and we only got . . . maybe a minute. But this is like . . ." She sent me a swift blue look that I couldn't read, grabbed her things, and ran into the change room.

I unpacked the Nikon, attached it to the lights with the cable. I'd be shooting at f 22, and the flash would be faster than any shutter speed, so Zoë could move as much as she wanted and so could I. Doc had left the lights in the classic forty-five degree setup, and I certainly wasn't about to try anything different. There was a small back light on the ceiling that would separate Zoë from the seamless. White fill cards were resting against the wall, but those were for head shots, so I wouldn't be needing them. It was a genuinely professional studio but simple enough for even a photographic idiot like me, and where was Zoë? In the change room, on the other side of the partition. I could hear her breathing. "Zo," I called to her, "you OK?"

"Sure. It's just . . . I can't . . . It's like, ah . . ."

I waited, but that seemed to be it. I stood there, baffled, in the patch of darkness just at the edge of the brilliant set. I listened to the rain muttering to itself. I could sense Zoë's misery radiating out from the change room like a force field, but I didn't know what to do about it, and then, with a sudden inner lurch, I lost all confidence in myself. What the hell was I doing? Playing a cut-rate version of John Hunt Morgan—trying to make a gesture as romantic as presenting a captured train to the local ladies? I imagined some hypothetical point in some hypothetical future when Revington and I might again have the luxury to piss away a few hours, drinking Irish whiskey and bullshitting each other, spinning a few more layers of legend around our already fabulous selves: "Well, yes, William, time was of the essence, but you know, man, before I left, I just needed to find . . . *something honorable*." And then what? I would gallop away into the sunset on my big white horse?

But Zoë wasn't playing a game. She was sixteen. The same age Cassandra had been when she and I had stood at the top of North High Street in Morgantown and read each other's minds. The same age I'd been when I'd shocked everybody by going out for track. And, with that, I felt again the full force of being sixteen— the tension, the ache, the despair of it—the sense of being caught in a fine mesh net, a tremendous power just beyond my reach, knowing that just thinking about it wouldn't get me anywhere, that I had to *do something*.

It didn't occur to me that a boy should not walk in on a girl in a change room until I'd already done it. Zoë was sitting motionless at the makeup table in front of a mirror ringed with bare light bulbs. She hadn't taken any of the rollers out of her hair. She was wearing nothing but Argyle tights with a bold diamond pattern and a plain white cotton bra. She looked up, and our eyes met in the mirror. "Are you OK?" I said.

I didn't know where she'd been—lost—but I saw her come back to *right now*, and then there was nothing we could possibly be except a boy and a girl alone together, and the boy had just caught the girl half dressed. The complex charge of that sexual polarity crackled between us—surprise, fear, confusion, embarrassment, maybe even, on some level, desire. I took a step backward. I was the wrong person in the wrong place. She didn't need a horny, terrified, phony Buddhist Confederate who'd just been drafted into the Yankee army; she needed a girlfriend. "Sorry," I said, "I was only . . ."

Then I stopped myself. No, it didn't have to be like that—I could feel it, the good, solid, useful energy of it. I had a choice to make, and I made it—allowed myself to step through a door in myself that had always been open. "What's the matter, Zoë" I said. "Do you want me to leave you alone? Is there any way I can help you? Tell me what to do."

She looked at me a moment longer, and I saw something change in her eyes. The polarity between us vanished into irrelevance like a card falling out of the deck; I swear we both felt it. "Oh, I'm such a little pin-brain," she said. "I should have . . . I don't know whether . . . I guess I should have put my sweater on first." She picked up the sponge she'd been using on her face and showed it to me as though it explained everything—and maybe it did. Her hand was shaking.

"That's foundation?" I said.

"Yeah. I've got to do my neck too or I'll look . . . you know, two-tone. I feel like such a little butterfingers today. I can't . . . Oh, I want to be so good!" She'd tried for her usual bright voice, but I heard a high wet trill to it—the edge of tears.

"I know," I said, and I did know. "You're going to be good." I reached for the sponge. She handed it to me. "What do I do?" I asked her.

"Just smooth it on and blend it in."

It was a shade lighter than her skin, so I could see what I'd done and what I hadn't. It blended in with hardly any effort. "Is this all right?" I said.

"Oh, yeah. It's great. You've got to do my ears too. You can look really ridiculous if you don't do your ears."

I did her ears and handed her the sponge. She looked at herself in the mirror, smoothed out a spot on her neck. I'd guessed that she was suffering from stage fright, and I knew from my days as a folk singer that there's a good kind and a bad kind of stage fright. The good kind makes you better—keys you up, makes you more alive. The bad kind makes you stupid and clumsy and slow. You get the bad kind when you're thinking about *yourself.* You get the good kind when you're thinking about *the music.* "I've always loved makeup," I said, "tell me how to do it."

"Oh! Do you really . . . ? OK. It's called *foundation* because that's what it is. It evens out your skin tone. Miss Fairfax says it's like an artist's canvas. Now I've got to put the color in."

My plan was working. She was coming out of her trance, the words beginning to tumble out of her again. She described everything she was doing: the color on her cheekbones, the lines around her lips and eyes, the complex layering of color on her eyelids. "It's got to look natural . . . if we're doing the cover of *Seventeen* . . . dewy and fresh and just *natural,* not like last time. I overdid it the last time, it's so hard to get the . . . you know, the ones in Cassandra's gown . . . the minute I saw the pictures, I knew, but it's so darned . . . you've got to put more on than in real life, for a photograph you do, but you've got to . . . 'Know when to stop, girls,' that's what Miss Fairfax always says, 'Restrain yourselves, girls.'"

I helped her on with the sweater that matched her tights—stretched the neck wide so she could slide her head through it without smudging her face. I fastened a plastic cape behind her neck so she could powder herself to "set" her artwork. I'd watched Cassandra take the rollers out of Zoë's hair, so I knew how to do it; Zoë didn't seem the least bit surprised that I'd taken over her sister's job. I loved the way each section sprang back into a perfect cylinder once I'd released it. When I was finished, she brushed herself out into a magazine-perfect pageboy. "It's easier for a picture," she said. "In real life it never stays like this longer than about five minutes."

She drew a red line around her lips with a pencil, filled in the line with lipstick applied with a sable brush. "This looks easy but it's not," she said. "It's got to be clean, but it can't look painted on." She curled her eyelashes and coated them with mascara—twice. She saw me studying her. "No, no," she said, "don't look *directly* at me. Miss Fairfax says when you're doing another girl's makeup, you always look at her in the mirror. Then you'll see what the camera's sees."

I stepped behind her and looked at her in the mirror. "Your eyeliner's a little smudgier on the left," I said.

"Oh, yeah." She blurred the line on her right eye until it matched. "Better?"

"Yeah. That's it."

"Oh, drat. Look. My mascara's clumped." She pointed. "Do you see it?"

I saw it. She rummaged in her tackle box, came up with a pin. "I hate this," she said. "It's really hard to do yourself."

"Do you want me to do it?"

She handed me the pin. "What am I supposed to do?"

"Just separate the lashes."

She sat perfectly still, staring straight ahead, holding her eyelids just slightly more than halfway open. I leaned toward her with the pin in my fingers, felt a momentary panic, but then that too dropped away. I'd never looked at anyone's eyelashes so closely before. They were not merely part of a decorative fringe cleverly designed to show off beautiful eyes; they were individual hairs, each growing out of sensitive living tissue. I inserted the pin into the clump of mascara at the base of her lashes—carefully, carefully—and stroked each lash clean.

"Oh, that's absolutely perfect," she said in a little voice as prim as Miss Muffet's. "Thank you so much."

"Oh, please don't mention it," I said. We both laughed.

She jumped up, lifted the short black vinyl skirt out of her suitcase, stepped into it. I zipped it up, smoothed it down to ride on her hip bones. "Don't you just love it?" she said.

"I love it."

"Me too." She did a pirouette, showing herself off.

"Zoë, you're a doll, you're a dream, you're perfect."

"Yeah, I am, aren't I?" Then her face fell as though some nasty inner voice had whispered: "Zoë, don't be stuck on yourself."

"It's OK to believe it," I said. "Go ahead and believe it. You've got to believe it."

She'd bought patent leather shoes to match the skirt; they were shaped like loafers but, like all of the girls' shoes in those days, cut tight to the foot and tapered to a gentle point. "Don't walk onto the seamless with your shoes on," I told her. "Put them on once you get there."

I looked at her through the lens. Under the modeling lights, her vinyl skirt caught the light and stated the superb lines of her hips. She stood, unmoving, waiting for me—willing herself to stand and wait. Her makeup was doing just what it was designed to do: her face really was as beautiful as a doll's—and just as blank. What we needed now was the charge, the kick of animal energy that would bring the doll to life. "You're wonderful," I said. "You're *better* than the cover of *Seventeen*," and there it was—that vital flash zapping straight at me from the center of her live eyes—and I hit the shutter. The lights fired with a deep thud. I heard her squeal. As the lights recycled, we were plunged for a moment into total darkness "Oh, my goodness," she said, breathing the words gently. "Boy, is this ever cool. This is so cool. It feels like for real."

"It is for real," I said.

WHEN WE got back to the house, Cassandra was sitting alone on the front porch glider. It was a perfectly ordinary thing for her to be doing, but finding her there shocked the hell out of me. I felt confused and undone—but no, that wasn't right. Startled, surprised, pole-axed, apprehensive, panicked, dismayed, appalled, God knows—I couldn't find words that were intense enough. To buy myself a second or two, I carefully set her father's camera case down by the door. "William told me," she said. "I'm so sorry."

Zoë was right behind me. "Mom's going to kill you," Cassandra said to her. "You should tell her when you're going to go play with John. She didn't have a clue."

"Yikes! I was going to leave her a note, but I must have forgot." Zoë ran inside, banging the door behind her. "Mom?" we heard her calling, "*Mommy? I'm home.*"

Cassandra reacted to *Mommy*—a thin smile and flick of the eyes that said, "Oh, she's such a little kid," inviting me to join her as a fellow grown-up, share the joke on little sister, but I was far from ready to do that. She must have read my expression as the deadpan stare of a just-drafted man; she stood up and put her arms around me. I hugged her back and squeezed. "Poor baby," she said. "I can't imagine you in the army."

"Yeah, I can't either."

"Do you want to talk about it?"

"I do, but not just yet."

We sat down on the glider. Cassandra was studying me. I was trying to keep my face neutral but didn't know whether I was succeeding or not. In the old days, she would have seen right through me. "Isn't it wonderful?" she said, gesturing toward the rain.

"Yeah," I said, "it's wonderful."

I must have jumped too quickly from little sister's world to big sister's; that's probably what it was—or at least that might explain some of my wretched feelings. I'd liked it so much in Zoë's world I'd almost forgotten that there was another one, but now I was back in Cassandra's world, and, I had to admit, it was my world too—a world of endless bombing raids and guys in jungles getting their asses shot off, of burning monks and burning children, of an insatiable draft that was gobbling up thirty-five thousand boys a month. Cassandra couldn't wear pink lipstick or a vinyl miniskirt in a world like that. No, she wore a boy's white shirt, tight jeans, flat beat-up shoes, dead white nails and lips, and fine black lines around her somber grey eyes. "Why didn't you call me, asshole?" she said.

"I did call you. Why aren't you ever home . . . *asshole?*"

She laughed. There was not much humor in it. "Your fucking friend," she said.

"*My* fucking friend?"

"Yeah, *your* fucking friend . . . Give me a cigarette."

I gave her one, lit one for myself. "OK, what about my fucking friend?"

"Shit. You know the night you got utterly plastered? Remember how Mom banished us to the back porch? And we were drinking that goddamn mint julep . . . I'll never touch that stuff again, believe me . . ."

I already knew how the story was going to unfold, but it was fascinating to hear it from Cassandra's point of view, and Zoë obviously wanted to hear it too; her face shiny with cold cream, she stepped quietly out onto the porch and settled onto one of the chairs. Her big sister sent her a complex look—an acknowledgement and a warning. "And then he's right behind me," Cassandra was saying, "and I turn around and he plants one on me. I mean tongue down my throat, the whole bit. God, I was shocked. And he says in one of his movie voices, 'Dear Cassandra, I've wanted to do that for years.' Like I'm . . . I don't know what. *Gigi*. And I'm thinking, oh, Jesus, when did I suddenly become irresistible?"

Zoë giggled. And it was funny, damn it. Really funny. Why wasn't I laughing?

"If he'd just knocked off the crap, if he'd just said something like, 'Look, Cass, I've been having a hell of a summer. Alicia's been in Europe since school was out, and I'm horny as hell, and I'm bored out of my mind, and you're probably horny as hell too, and bored out of your mind, and we're obviously attracted to each other, so why don't we go to bed?' I probably would have said, 'Sure, why not?' But that's not what he said. Oh, Jesus. Do you want to know what he did?"

Because I knew him, I could guess easily enough what he'd done, but I let her tell me all about it—the intimate dinners at the country club, the nights at the movies, the walks in the park, the drive to Pittsburgh to see the ballet. I already knew I'd won the bet, and the more she told me, the more ashamed I felt. For years I'd believed that she was closer to me than anybody, so what had I been trying to do, get her to prove it?

"OK," she said, "so what the hell does he *want?* Well, it's obvious what he wants, but *why?* I'm pretty sure he doesn't even like me all that much, and I'm thinking, all right, William, let's just see how far you're going to run with this one . . ."

Cassandra's assessment was right on the money. He *didn't* like her all that much; he thought she was an arrogant little bitch who needed "a good, thorough, methodical, therapeutic screwing," quote, unquote. But I didn't need to tell her about the goddamned bet, did I? If I told her, I'd be ratting on my friend and hurting her to no good purpose, so I should keep my mouth shut, laugh in the right places, play out my own drama, shuffle off into the wings as the curtain went down, and she'd be none the wiser. Didn't I have the right to do that? My life was changing forever. By this time tomorrow, none of these silly games would matter a damn.

"And when we were having our little tête-à-têtes," Cassandra was saying, "do you know what he talked about? *Himself.* For hours."

"Oh, no," I said.

"Oh, yes. And you can see where all this is going, right? His dad's at work and his mom's at some damn meeting of some damn society you belong to if you're Mrs. Revington, and we're alone in the house. And do you know what he's doing? Jesus. He's handing me this huge load of shit, this unbelievable snow job. He wants me to feel sorry for him. Him, of all people! Staring off into space, all this crap about how he's going to be in uniform by Christmas and probably get himself killed over there. And all of a sudden it just makes me sick. So I say, 'I think you better take me home now, William. I don't feel very well. I must have got too much sun.'"

"He didn't try the one about the baby?"

"What?"

"How he wanted to leave something honorable behind him after he went *over there* . . . a *baby*?"

"Oh, Jesus."

"Cassandra," I said, "it was a bet."

"What?"

"He bet me a bottle of Scotch he could screw you by the end of the summer."

Zoë emitted a small strangled yelp. "You just shut up, twinkle toes," Cassandra snapped at her. "You shouldn't even be hearing this shit."

I looked at Cassandra's profile. She was staring at a fixed point somewhere out in the street where the rain was falling. It was the kind of undistinguished rain that felt eternal. I looked at Zoë. I was afraid of what she might be thinking of me, but she sent me a sympathetic glance and a barely perceptible flicker of a gesture, one I read as: "Come on, *say something!*" Yeah, right, but what could I say?

"You prick," Cassandra said, still not looking at me, "what are you doing, making bets on my ass?"

"Just like everything else," I said, "it was supposed to be a joke. I don't know what's happened to us, I honest to God don't."

"Oh, it's funny all right. Of course it's funny. You goddamned vermin, you almost got me good." She turned and looked into my eyes.

This was not the existentially flattened, jaded, bored and bitter girl she'd been presenting to me since I'd come home. This was a girl I'd hurt. "I'm sorry," I said.

"Guess what, Dupre? You bastards owe *me* a bottle of Scotch."

"Sure," I said. "That's fair enough. Maybe he'll even think it's funny."

I only wished that a bottle of Scotch would do it—restore the essential sense of balance, of proportion, that must have slipped away from us over the summer. Maybe I shouldn't have told her. Maybe I'd just ruined everything. Events kept outstripping my punch lines, and now I seemed to be stuck with my own chain of causality—with nothing left to do but follow it out, step by step.

But it was *painful*, damn it—and I'd been making a series of evasive maneuvers to save myself from having to feel how painful it was. When I'd walked up onto the porch and found Cassandra there, what I'd seen had been the gravity of my own life, and this time it wasn't a poetic flight of fancy but literally the truth: I might never be back here again. I knew how easily I could turn it all into lies and nostalgia—remembering this porch, this glider, this rain, these girls, putting names to it like "dear" and "lost," and I didn't want to do that. I wanted to remember it as it was—the annoying squeak of the glider, Zoë's shiny clean face and Cassandra's dark one, the light, the pause, the breath, the pearly grey, the rain, the rain, the rain. Oh, my God, I was leaving.

COME ON, DUPRE, THAT'S ENOUGH OF THAT. WRAP THINGS UP. Well, yes, I could do that. But I needed Revington. I'd written him into the last act. "Where the hell is he?" I said. "It's not like him to miss his cue."

"Who? William?"

"Yeah, *William.* I'm damned near out of time, for Christ's sake. I'm leaving tomorrow, for Christ's sake. What's he waiting for? Call him up and tell him to get his sorry ass over here."

Cassy called him, and Revington arrived in less than ten minutes. He pulled up in front of the house and stepped out of his car. He was wearing a highly improbable fedora. He walked purposefully toward the porch but then stopped abruptly and stood stock still in the rain. Scowling, he stared up at the ceiling above our heads. *Wonderful,* I thought. I knew exactly what he was doing. It was perfect. "Say there, buddy," he yelled at me, "why don't you fix that leak in your roof?"

I squinched a yokel's bemusement onto my face, cast my eyes upward, furrowed my brow, and studied the imaginary leak. "Hell," I yelled back at him, "I can't fix the roof when it's raining."

"Well, why don't you fix it when the sun comes out?"

"When the sun comes out . . ." I said to Cassandra, shaking my head, mugging my amazement at the idiocy of this stranger who had suddenly appeared at my shack. "When the sun comes out . . ." I repeated to Zoë to make her giggle. Then I turned back to Revington: "Mister, you *are* a fool. When the sun comes out, the roof don't leak."

"Drum roll," Cassy said. "Cymbal crash . . . God, you guys are pathetic."

Revington stepped up onto the porch and offered his hand. I rose to my feet, grabbed it and squeezed. "How you doing, ace?" he said.

"Not half bad."

"When are you leaving?"

"Tomorrow."

I sat down again on the glider. He settled into a chair. "Do you have any idea where you'll be stationed?" he asked me.

"Wait a minute," I said. William Revington wasn't the only one with a flair for the dramatic. I pulled the envelope out of my jeans and threw it to Cassandra. I'd been saving it for precisely this moment: my joker from the bottom of the deck.

"What's this?" She opened the envelope, looked inside, and laughed. There was no bitterness in that laugh, only delight—a sound as clean as the rain. Of course we were linked. We always had been and always would be. It was stronger than if we'd been lovers.

Grinning, Cassandra handed the envelope to her little sister. It took Zoë a moment to get it; then her lips silently said, "cool," and she passed it on to Revington.

He frowned, passed it back to me: my one-way ticket to Toronto. His eyes were as hurt as if I'd done some terrible thing directly to him. ASK NOT WHAT YOUR COUNTRY CAN DO FOR YOU. "You'll be back," he said.

"No, I won't," I said.

Author's Afterword

This, the third volume of the *Difficulty at the Beginning* quartet, bears no direct relationship to the story of John Dupre's life in the summer of 1965 that was published under the title of "South" as the first half of *Cutting Through* (General Publishing, Toronto, 1982). Although I did manage to salvage roughly four pages of material from "South," I based this book entirely on an unpublished short story (now housed in the archives at the University of British Columbia library) that I wrote in the early 1970s; I kept the original title—*Lyndon Johnson and the Majorettes*—thoroughly rewrote the story, added many new elements to it, and expanded it to approximately five times its original length. I consider this book to be a new work.

References to T. S. Eliot's "The Waste Land" were always present in the earliest drafts of the short story. Playing with literary devices that were all the rage when John was in university, I have amplified the relationship between Eliot's text and mine, but I have tried to do so in a way that is unobtrusive. I offer my efforts in the same spirit with which John offers his toast to Eliot: "Here's to you, master of the mug's game."

Lyndon's Johnson's speech to the nation was widely reprinted in the newspapers of the time. The cover of *Seventeen* that Zoë imitates in the photo shoot at the end of the book is that of August, 1965 (the same issue that she and John flip through earlier in the story). Except for my sketch of John Hunt Morgan and the mention of well-known public figures such as the ubiquitous president from Texas, none of the characters in this book are real. The summer of 1965, however, is just as real as I could make it.

Keith Maillard, Vancouver, January 12, 2006

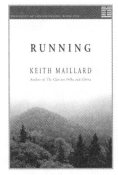 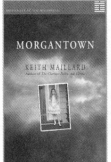 

The *Difficulty at the Beginning* quartet follows John Dupre from his awkward high-school years in the late 1950s through the burgeoning counterculture movement of the early 1960s to the tumultuous and devastating late-1960s political and psychedelic underground.

Each of the four volumes is written in the style of the times. In *Running* the façade of post-WWII American optimism is just beginning to crack. *Morgantown* hums and throbs with the freewheeling energy and free-floating angst of youth pushing against the boundaries of social acceptability. *Lyndon Johnson and the Majorettes* situates the anxiety of the years following Kennedy's assassination and the impending threat of the Vietnam draft in the oppressive heat of a West Virginia summer. In the final volume, *Looking Good*, all the currents of the high sixties draw together in an explosive climax.

By any measure, *Difficulty at the Beginning* is a major addition to American and Canadian literature, a brilliant and supremely readable social chronicle that ranks with the best of North American fiction.

RUNNING • 1-897142-06-4 • SEPTEMBER 2005

MORGANTOWN • 1-897142-07-2 • FEBRUARY 2006

LYNDON JOHNSON AND THE MAJORETTES • 1-897142-08-0 • APRIL 2006

LOOKING GOOD • 1-897142-09-9 • SEPTEMBER 2006

BOOKS BY KEITH MAILLARD

Novels

Two Strand River (1976)

Alex Driving South (1980)

The Knife in My Hands (1981)

Cutting Through (1982)

Motet (1989)

Light in the Company of Women (1993)

Hazard Zones (1995)

Gloria (1999)

The Clarinet Polka (2002)

Difficulty at the Beginning

    Book 1: *Running* (2005)

    Book 2: *Morgantown* (2006)

    Book 3: *Lyndon Johnson and the Majorettes* (2006)

    Book 4: *Looking Good* (2006)

Poetry

Dementia Americana (1995)